Boy Meets Boy

Boy Meets Boy

Copyright © 2023 by Jake Uniacke

All rights reserved.

Paperback ISBN: 9798854586870

No portion of this book may be reproduced in any form without written permission from the publisher or author, except as permitted by UK copyright law.

Boy Meets Boy

JAKE UNIACKE

Also by Jake Uniacke
Lighthouse
The Girl From Under The Water
The King's Army

Part 1

Danny

I'VE WANTED TO BE a photographer ever since I left school. There is just something magical about telling a story through a photograph. I love taking photos of people - my friends have been models for me in the past, posing in different positions and pulling different facial expressions to really portray the emotion of the story I want to tell. Now, I sit in front of the managing director for a huge magazine in London.

"So, tell me a bit about yourself," she says.

I pause for a moment, frozen with panic. I always hate having to talk about myself, I never know what to say. I gather myself and then proceed to answer the question. "I suppose I'm a bit of a geek. Photography plays a huge part of my life, it's something I've been incredibly passionate about for a good three years now. I'm an extremely creative person, and when I'm not doing anything remotely creative, I like to go on bike rides with my dad. He's very sporty and he got me into some of the different sports I like such as cycling and golf."

Stacey Cheng, the managing director of *Rainbow Magazine*, nods and smiles. She takes a few notes and then looks back at me. "What is it about photography that you enjoy so much? Where did the passion come from?"

An easy question for me to answer. "It started back in school. We did a photography project in an media lesson- we had to analyse a photograph, think of what the photographer was trying to portray, and then recreate the photo with the objects and people we had around us. Ever since I got a B in my GCSE exam for that, I figured that photography would be the path I want to go down."

I'm quite impressed with my answer - it's very rare that I actually feel confident about an interview. But Stacey is giving me positive vibes about this and I'm not about to let anything get in my way of achieving my dreams. Even if I give a shit answer to a question, I want Stacey to know that I'm very confident in myself and I'm the best person for this apprenticeship.

Stacey looks to her left, where her colleague, Jamie-Lee Parks, is sitting. She's the publicity manager for the magazine, and wants to make sure they have the very best photographers for the job. After all, taking photos for a magazine is a very full on job as the photos have to be in pristine quality and suitable for printing. The reader - predominantly gay men - have to be able to see what the photographer is portraying in the photo. They have to *feel* the emotion behind the story being told on the page. Jamie-Lee looks towards me and asks how I think *I* would be able to represent the stories that these men tell in the magazine.

I think back to a story I read in an edition of *Rainbow Magazine* I bought a few months ago. It was written by a man aged sixty-three and had only come out three months prior to the story being published. He wrote about how his wife was surprised but was fully accepting and to this day, are still the best of friends. The story was beautiful and I admit that I actually teared up a little bit when I read it. The photograph of him was the saddest yet happiest thing I had ever seen. It was black and white, representing his generation, and he had the biggest smile on his face. He was finally able to be himself and I felt that the photographer portrayed his story in the most perfect way.

I realise I have zoned out and I turn my attention back to Stacey and Jamie-Lee. "Sorry, I was just reminiscing on a previous story you published a while ago. It's actually very relevant and I'm going to use it as an example if that's okay." I relay the story to the two women sitting in front of me, and they nod, clearly remembering every detail of that man's story. "If I was the photographer for that man, I honestly wouldn't have changed a thing that Frankie Ginola did. He portrayed Mr Withers' story perfectly and the photo was absolutely beautiful. I'm a *huge* fan of Ginola's work and he is actually one of my earliest inspirations. His style is something that I don't want to copy, but rather take bits from and put my own twist on it."

Stacey and Jamie-Lee, once again, nod and smile. I think they're impressed with me. I really hope so - this apprenticeship will mean everything to me.

"Thank you for your time, Danny," says Stacey, "we really appreciate you coming in and it has been lovely to hear about you and your love for photography. Do you have any questions for us?"

I think for a moment. I'm not great at asking questions when prompted on the spot. But, I manage to conjure up a question anyway.

"When working with the models, what is your ideal process for a photographer to go through?" I ask.

Jamie-Lee takes the question. "We like our photographers to go through whichever process they see fit for *them*. We won't tell you to do this or to do that, you'll do what you feel is right under the guidance of our photography director."

I'm pleased with that answer. I would *hate* to be told how to take a photo or which angle to shoot from. I'm my own person, I have my own style and the way I visualise things will obviously be completely different to the people who work here.

"I think that's the only question I have," I say. "Thank you so much for seeing me, it's been a pleasure to meet you."

"You too, Danny," Stacey says. "We'll be in touch in the next couple of days after we've completed a few more interviews. Take care."

I say goodbye and then leave the office. I walk out of the building with a great big smile on my face. I'm *really* happy with the way that interview went. I just hope they saw the real me and think I'm perfect for the role.

·♥·♥·♥·♥·♥·

My phone buzzes on my bedside table, waking me up from my sleep. I jolt awake and look at who is phoning. It's not a number I recognise, but I answer it anyway.

"Hello?" I say.

"Hello, it's Stacey?" a lady on the other end of the phone replies.

"Oh, hi Stacey!"

"I just wanted to phone you to let you know that we would, in fact, like to offer you the apprenticeship as a Junior Photographer."

I let out an internal excited scream. "Oh my goodness! Thank you so much."

Stacey giggles. "We would like you to come back for a follow up chat, just to finalise everything and get the paperwork signed etcetera. When is suitable for you?"

Stacey and I chat for a few minutes on the phone and then we end the conversation. I'm so excited. I *knew* I wouldn't have to go to university to get into photography. I'm about to prove my college lecturer *wrong*.

I race downstairs, darting towards the kitchen where my parents are busy preparing dinner. The smell of bolognese fills my nostrils with a delightful scent, and my stomach rumbles like a thunderstorm. I stand in the doorway, a great big grin on my face. My mother turns around from the stove and looks at me, confusion written all over her face. She smiles and my father looks up from the newspaper he is reading.

"What are you smiling about?" Mum asks.

I clear my throat. "Stacey Cheng from *Rainbow Magazine* just called. She wants to offer me the apprenticeship. I'm moving to London!"

Mum jumps up and down with joy, screaming with pride as she runs over to me to give me a hug, bolognese sauce dripping down her apron and transferring to my jumper. She pulls away and gives me a massive kiss on the forehead. Dad stays where he is and just says a very underwhelming "Well done."

"I am *so* proud of you!" screams Mum. "You've worked so hard for this, you fully deserve it." She pulls her apron over her head and turns off the stove. "Stuff the bolognese. We're going out for dinner tonight to celebrate. Your father's treat."

Dad shoots Mum a look of despair. "Why my treat? You suggested it."

"Because Danny is your son and he deserves a treat. Plus, you don't seem very proud of him."

"Of course I'm proud of him. I just don't feel happy with him going all the way to London away from us."

Mum rolls her eyes. "Not everything is about you, Dave. As his parents, we have to support him in every single way."

I tut. "Don't argue about it, please. I'm more than happy with bolognese here at home. Anyway, I need to see Ellie tonight and tell her the news. I don't want to text her it, I want to tell her face to face."

Mum smiles. "Of course. How is she doing?"

"Yeah, she's doing well. The surgery was a success and she can finally be herself."

"That's good. I'm so pleased her transition is going well. She's been such a good friend to you all these years and deserves happiness."

I sit down at the dining table with Dad and pull my phone from my pocket. I give Ellie a text to let her know I'm coming round tonight and then pluck a few grapes from the fruit bowl in the centre of the table.

"So, what does this apprenticeship entail?" my dad asks, not showing an ounce of interest.

"I'll be photographing models for the magazine and any men that come to the magazine with their story. It seems so exciting," I explain, "but it's going to be hard work."

"Taking photos? That's not exactly hard work."

I roll my eyes. "There's a lot more to it than you think, it's not just clicking a button and being done with it. There's so much to-"

Dad cuts me off with a loud yawn. "Sorry, son. You're boring me."

I frown and look down at the table. My dad has never been one for showing me any love - in fact, his attitude started from the moment I came out as gay. He doesn't like me going to work for an LGBTQIA+ magazine - it makes him feel *uncomfortable* apparently.

"Dave, stop it!" Mum snaps. "Danny is finally chasing his dreams and all you can do is sit there and insult him. You are a *terrible* father."

Dad gets up from the table and stomps out of the kitchen and heads to the living room. Mum sits down next to me and takes my hands.

"Don't listen to him," she says. "He's a dick."

I chuckle, but can't help but make my sadness obvious. "Why are you still with him, Mum?"

Mum sighs and shrugs. "Honestly, I don't know. He treats you so poorly, yet I still love him to pieces. We met when we were in college, so we're soulmates."

"But he's homophobic. He hates me."

"He doesn't hate you." Mum pulls me into a tight embrace. "He's just struggling to get his head around it, that's all."

"There isn't anything *to* get his head around. This is who I am, I'm still his son."

"I know." Mum pulls away. "But your father is very old fashioned. He doesn't know how to show affection to many people. To be honest, his levels of affection towards *me* have fizzled down over the years."

"But you're not gay."

Mum frowns and holds my hand tightly again. "I know, and I'm *so* sorry that he treats you this way. Maybe going to London will be the best thing for you. A clean break, new friends and you'll meet a whole new community who will accept you for who you are. And I will *always* be on the other end of the phone if you need me."

"Thanks, Mum."

Mum kisses me and then hurries back over to the stove to stir the pasta. Getting away from Dad will be the best thing, it means I no longer have to put up with his attitude towards me. I can finally be me without the fear of being ridiculed by my own father.

Danny

I PARK UP OUTSIDE Ellie's house and wander up the garden path towards her front door. The garden is presented beautifully, flowers blooming from the shrubs and small statues dotted around the lawn. I knock the front door and wait a few seconds before the door finally opens. Ellie stands in the doorway, gleaming as she sees me.

"Hey," she says, "you okay?"

I nod and she invites me inside. We head up to her bedroom and she closes the curtains as the sun begins to set. I turn on the light. We sit together on her bed and she offers me one of her chocolate hobnobs that she's been stashing in her drawer. I take one and tuck into it.

"So, I've got some news," I say.

Ellie swallows her biscuit before speaking. "Go on."

"You know that apprenticeship I applied for in London for the *Rainbow Magazine*? Well, the managing director called me earlier today and offered me the role. I'm moving to London!"

Ellie doesn't react in the way I was hoping she would, but rather in the way I *expected* her to. Instead of throwing herself at me in a proud hug and screaming in my ear about how pleased she is for me, she slouches down on the bed and sadness takes over her entire face. I wish she would be pleased for me, it seems my mum is the only person I've got right now who is proud of me.

"You are happy for me, aren't you?" I ask.

Ellie nods. "Of course I am. I'm just disappointed that it's so far away."

"It's only a couple of hours on the train. Besides, I'll be coming back every other weekend so I'm *sure* we will see each other. I'll make sure of it."

I can tell that Ellie isn't completely convinced by this, and I can kind of understand why. A few years ago, she had a friend called Nancy and they had formed such a close relationship. When Nancy announced she was moving to Basingstoke, she promised to visit Ellie at least once a month. At first, it started off well. Then, once a month turned into once every couple of months. And then that turned into never, and they eventually drifted apart. They're not in touch anymore. Ellie is obviously scared the same thing is going to happen between us, but

I want her to know that that *isn't* the case and I'll always be here for her.

"I promise," I say before she can say anything, "that I'll make time for you. You're my best friend and you've been there for me through some of my toughest times. I'd never abandon you."

"Promise?" Ellie whimpers.

"Cross my heart."

Ellie leans forward and hugs me as tight as she can. My friendship with Ellie means the world to me, and I can't imagine my life without her in it, so I have to stick to my word. It's going to be hard trying to see her *and* my family. But I'll do whatever I can to make it work.

·♥·♥·♥·♥·♥·

It's 9pm when I leave Ellie's house. On my way home, I stop off at the small corner shop just down the road from my house to buy myself some snacks, and some flowers for my mum. She's been there for me and she's the only person who has shown an ounce of pride, so I want to show her my appreciation with these flowers.

"Do you have any roses?" I ask the shopkeeper, Robbie. I'm a regular in the shop, so we know each other by name. "They're my mum's favourite."

"Chocolates or flowers?" Robbie asks.

I chuckle. "Flowers. Although, I suppose the chocolates will do if you don't have any flowers." I wink at him, and we both have a little laugh together.

Robbie checks the flower stall, but comes back with no roses. "Sorry buddy," he says. "I do have an offer on the boxes of the *Roses* chocolates, though. Two for five pounds."

I pull my wallet out and hand over a five pound note. Robbie takes it and I pick up two boxes of *Roses* from the counter. I thank Robbie and then leave the shop. Mum doesn't need *two* boxes of chocolates, so I decide I'm going to give one to Ellie as a goodbye gift.

As I park up on the driveway, I notice my dad in the garage. I wander over to him and ask what he's doing.

"I'm building a mini studio for you," he says. He looks around at the mess and the crappy bits of wood that haven't sawed properly. "Well, I'm trying to."

I smile and slightly tear up. It's the most thoughtful thing my dad has ever done for me since I came out. "Why are you doing this?"

"Because you're my son, and I love you. And I'm sorry. You make me *so* proud, and I am honestly so happy for you for getting this job. It's what you've always wanted."

"Thanks, Dad."

I hug him tight and then head indoors. Mum is relaxing on the sofa, book in her hands and her hair wrapped in her fluffy pink towel.

"Hiya, love," she says.

"Hi, Mum," I reply. "These are for you. Thank you for everything you do for me." I hand her the box of chocolates and she smiles at me.

"You didn't have to get these!" She stands up and hugs me, her damp towel around her head pressing against my face. I wipe the dampness from my face with my jumper.

"You've done so much for me, and I want to show my appreciation. I know it isn't much but-"

"Shush," she says, interrupting me. "I will *always* do what I can to protect you. Now, go and get into your pyjamas and we'll watch that movie you like."

I rush off to my bedroom and change into my Disney pyjamas, before heading back downstairs and setting up the *Pitch Perfect* DVD on the TV. It finally feels as though I've got *both* parents on my side. And I'll be forever grateful for that.

·♥·♥·♥·♥·♥·

I wake up to my alarm screaming in my ear. It's Saturday morning and the sun shines through my bedroom window, the curtains not doing a great job at stopping the light from coming through. I bat my eyelids a few times before opening them fully and coming to terms with the fact that it is a new day.

I pick my phone up from my bedside table and open a text message from Ellie.

When do you start your apprenticeship? X

I type out a reply. *Hopefully at the start of September!* X

With September just a couple of weeks away, I get my hopes up that everything will fall into place and I'll get my apprenticeship off to a good start as soon as possible. The college I'm going to be attending alongside the apprenticeship is having an open day on Tuesday for new students, so I've decided I'm going to go along to it just to see where I'll be learning and meeting my lecturer.

Just as I climb out of bed, my phone rings. It's Ellie.

"Hey," I say after I've swiped the small green phone icon.

"Hey," replies Ellie, "do you want to do something today? We should celebrate your apprenticeship."

"Yeah that would be great. What're you thinking?" I'm curious as Ellie always comes up with these weird and wonderful ideas for plans that I think are absolutely ridiculous.

"Maybe we could go bowling and have a meal out. We can also invite the others from our group chat."

I nod. "Yeah, that sounds brilliant. Do you want to put something in the chat and I'll get ready to come out?"

"Yep, perfect." Ellie hangs up and seconds later, my phone pings with a message from Ellie to our group chat, conveniently called *The Rainbow Brigade* since we all identify as a member of the LGBTQIA+ community. It's our little joke, meant to mock the homophobes who use that term as a way of insulting us. Instead though, we just laugh.

I put my phone in my dressing gown pocket as I head into the kitchen and pour myself a bowl of cereal. Mum and Dad are still in bed, so I head into the living room to eat breakfast whilst watching a TV show I recorded on the Sky box last night. I tuck into my cereal, the milk dripping from the spoon and down my chin. I wipe my chin with a tissue from the box on the coffee table and then finish off the bowl.

Everyone seems to be awake early as my phone keeps pinging, messages flying into the group chat every few seconds, all my friends agreeing to a day of bowling and food. This could be the last time I see my friends for a while if things go smoothly with this apprenticeship as I rarely see these guys anymore. So, I just hope I can make the most of today and we all have a great time.

·♥·♥·♥·♥·♥·

We arrive at the bowling alley at around 12pm. and purchase our games. We're told our alley will be about a ten minute wait, so we grab a couple of drinks from the bar and then sit on the sofa, waiting for the family on Alley 6 to finish their game. Of everyone in the group chat who said they *would* come along today, only *four* actually turned up. Richard, Ollie, Lydia, and Freddie gather around me and give me a massive hug, congratulating me on the apprenticeship. Ellie sits awkwardly, but jumps up as soon as Alley 6 becomes free again.

"Come on guys," says Ellie, "let's go bowling!"

We head over to the alley and put our drinks down on the table. I input everyone's names onto the system, putting us in an order of play. I'm up first, followed by Ellie, then Richard, then Lydia, then Ollie, and finally Freddie. We decided to play in a boy-girl order, Freddie being the exception due to their gender identity, to make it fair and equal.

I pick up a medium sized orange bowling ball and position myself at a certain angle that I want to throw the ball. I aim the ball straight down the middle of the alley, watching it roll along the waxed wooden surface before finally hitting the pins, knocking down seven and leaving three standing.

"So *close*!" Richard yelled. "You can get a spare!"

I pick up another ball and concentrate hard as I launch the ball down the alley again and watch it hit the three remaining bowling pins. *Spare!*

My friends cheer and then Ellie takes her position at the end of the alley with the ball she has chosen. She gets a strike immediately.

"Cheat!" I yell, jokingly.

Ellie pokes her tongue out at me. "You're just jealous that you're shit at bowling."

"Oh yeah? We'll see about that - there's still nine more rounds."

We both chuckle as Richard makes his way over to the alley. I take a sip of my drink and smile as I watch my friends have fun. It's been so long since we all got together like this and had a laugh. And now, it's going to be a while again. I'm so lucky to have such an amazing group of friends.

Our game of bowling comes to an end and overall, Ellie ended up winning. She's always been good at bowling. Our joke is that despite the majority of our group being gay, she's the best when it comes to handling balls. She never appreciated that joke before her transition, but she's learned to appreciate it and since then, has always laughed along with us.

We head off to the restaurant next door to the bowling alley and the waiter shows us to our table. We each choose a seat and then pick up a menu each and read through it, browsing the selection of delicious meal choices.

"Shall we get some drinks in?" I ask. "What would everyone like?"

Everyone tells me they'd like an alcoholic drink, except for Lydia as she's driving - so at least I'm not alone with that as I'm not drinking either. I walk up to the bar, order everyone's drinks and then head back to the table with a tray full of glasses and bottles. I pass everyone their chosen drink and then sit back down in my seat.

"Thanks for coming today," I say, "it's been really special."

Everyone smiles at me and congratulates me once again on my apprenticeship. It's been an odd day - hanging out with everyone I've not seen for a few months - but it has been great fun and has been lovely to see everyone again.

"We'll have to come up to London to visit you," says Richard, "and see what you're getting up to. Hopefully you'll find yourself a nice boyfriend at your job, too."

I chuckle. "That's unlikely."

·♥··♥·♥·♥·♥·

As our day out together comes to a close, I give everyone a hug and thank them once again for coming along and making today fun and special. Ellie tears up a little bit, and I take her aside to ask her what's wrong.

"Just this," she says. "Today has been so much fun and I'm just so sad that this will be the last time we do this for a long time."

I hold her hand. "I will make sure we do something like this *at least* once a month. I'll need some sort of escape from my family every once in a while."

"Do you promise?"

"I double promise."

She smiles and hugs me again. Ellie is going to be the person I find it hardest to say goodbye to. After all, she has been my best friend since we were little so we've grown up together. She's been there for me through thick and thin, so saying goodbye and not seeing her as often will be extremely difficult.

The others head off their separate ways, and I offer Ellie a lift home. We jump in the car and head off down the road towards her house. I pull up outside Ellie's house and we sit in the car for a couple of minutes, talking about everything. Ellie starts to cry again so I pull her into a hug and reassure her that everything will be okay and I'll be down every other weekend, and I will phone her or video call her at every opportunity I get. There is absolutely no way I will be abandoning her. Once I'm satisfied that Ellie is happy and reassured, I let her go and I drive off home, waving as I pull away from Ellie's driveway.

I arrive home a short while later, after taking a detour along the seafront. The next couple of weeks are going to be spent preparing to move to London, so I'm not going to get the chance to come to the beach much and take in the beautiful view. I used to come here all the time as a child. Mum and Dad would bring me here every weekend during the summer to play in the sea and build sandcastles, and during the winter, we would come here for a walk every Sunday morning no matter how cold or wet it was. There are so many memories at this beach and I'm actually quite sad to say goodbye to them.

I sit down at the kitchen table with a glass of water and check my emails. Stacey Cheng has emailed me, letting me know that they're currently processing my accommodation arrangements and have found me a studio flat about a twenty minute drive from the studio. That's perfect for me, that's all I need really. I swipe through the photos she sent me and the flat doesn't look too shabby. Yes, it's small, but it's only me living there and I'll only be eating and sleeping there. I respond to Stacey's email to let her know I'm happy with the flat and she can go ahead with the process - not that I had much choice in the first place. With such short notice for this apprenticeship, I will have to take what I can get.

Mum struts into the kitchen and leans over me, hugging me tight and giving me a big kiss on the cheek. "How was your afternoon out?"

"It was so much fun," I say. "Ellie won the bowling - no surprise there - and I had the *best* dessert after our meal."

Mum sounds jealous. "What did you have?"

My mouth waters just thinking about it. "Banoffee pie with caramel *and* vanilla ice cream."

"Oh my goodness, that sounds *incredible*."

I smile. "Oh, it was!"

Stacey replies to my email quickly, and I open it immediately.

Dear Danny,

Thank you for your prompt reply. I am so pleased you like the studio flat. I'm just awaiting confirmation from the estate agent that the property is ready to move into. We will cover the rent for the duration of your apprenticeship, and then if we decide to take you on permanently, you will have to start paying the rent.

I'm also pleased to inform you that I can officially confirm that you can start on Monday 9th September. As stated in the job description, you'll be working 9am-5pm, Monday to Friday. Please arrive at the location of your flat by Friday 6th September so you can start getting settled.

Please let me know if you have any questions and I look forward to seeing you in a couple of weeks!

Warmest regards,

Stacey Cheng

Managing Director of Rainbow Magazine

I can't believe it. I'm moving to London at the end of *next week*!

Harry

I STARE AT THE piece of paper that was just presented in front of me - a contract. I read through the long paragraphs, taking in all of the words and trying my best to understand what they all mean. As I reach the end of the contract, I see where I must sign. I hesitate for a few seconds, unsure if I'm making the right decision. But looking at Stacey's big grin on her face and her positive eyes, I put pen to paper and scribble my signature on the line where I'm required to sign.

"Perfect," says Stacey, taking the contract from me and slipping it into a folder. "You'll meet your fellow apprentice when you both start, and just to clarify what it says in the contract, only one of you will be taken on permanently at the end of the apprenticeship."

"So, it's almost like a competition?" I ask.

"Kind of but not quite, if that makes sense? You're competing for the same job but it isn't a rivalry."

This doesn't sit right with me, but I guess this is the real world. I nod in agreement.

⋅♥⋅♥⋅♥⋅♥⋅♥⋅

"How did it go?" Mum asks when I arrive home.

I don't smile. In fact, I just huff. "It doesn't sit right with me. Stacey said that I'll be up against *another* apprentice in the *same* role and fighting for the permanent job. I already knew that the apprenticeship is for two people but I didn't realise it is essentially a competition."

"That's not right. An apprenticeship is all about learning and becoming more confident in what you want to do. Did she say *why* this is the case?"

"No. I just went with it. I enjoy photography and modelling so maybe I'll get the opportunity to do both there. And, even if I don't get the job as a photographer after the apprenticeship, I might be able to stay on and model?"

I can see Mum isn't too sure and that I'm probably getting ahead of myself, but she clearly doesn't want to burst my bubble.

⋅♥⋅♥⋅♥⋅♥⋅♥⋅

I browse through some of the photographs I've taken over the last couple of months, proud with the result and proud of myself. These days, it's rare that I manage to capture a good photo, especially since my passion for photography fizzled out when my grandfather passed away. He was my biggest supporter and always loved seeing what I had photographed, whether it was nature, wildlife, or people, and when he passed, photography was the last thing on my mind.

I look at the photo I took of my uncle. He's standing in his back garden, shovel in one hand and his other hand on his hip. On that photoshoot, I asked him to pose as if he was a gardener - in some ways he is, with the way he looks after his allotment and helps his wife turn the garden into a beautiful landscape. This is probably one of my favourite photos, and I showed it to Stacey Cheng during my interview as part of my portfolio. She seemed really impressed with it, and loved the way I directed my uncle to make sure I captured a wonderful photo.

Mum enters my bedroom after knocking and comes over to look at my photos with me. "I always loved that one of your father," she says as I click onto the next photo which shows my dad acting like he'd just had his heart broken. I had asked him to pretend Mum had just dropped a bombshell and I wanted to capture his reaction. And, he did it rather well. Ever since that photoshoot, my mum has always said it is one of her favourite photos I've taken because it really pulls at the heartstrings - and she's never seen my dad like that before (he's never been great at showing his emotions).

"I'm thinking about setting up an Instagram page for my photography," I say. "Obviously, I have my personal page and I post some of my photos on there but I want the *world* to see what I can do and not just my friends and the family."

"I think that's a brilliant idea, Harry," says Mum. "Just make sure you ask those people for permission first. They may not want you to plaster their faces all over the internet."

I nod my head. "I know, thanks Mum."

Mum leaves my room, allowing me to browse through my photos in peace. And then, I come across that *one* photo I always love to look at - my college crush. It's not a creepy, sneaky photo. I asked if I could take a photo of him when he was in the gym as part of my action shot portfolio. He agreed, and after I saw him in his gym gear, I just couldn't get him out of my head. Ever since that photoshoot, he had approached me several times in college to do more photoshoots to the point where we were hanging out in the gym every other day whilst I took photos and he worked out. But this photo - this one is my favourite. I stare at my computer screen as this guy's toned body fills my screen, his biceps bulging as he lifts the barbell from the ground. Despite me soon finding out he had a girlfriend, my crush on him never fizzled out. But I felt it was appropriate to stop hanging around with him and I told him I didn't want to do action shots anymore - obviously, that was a lie.

Ever since I met him though, I grew a huge interest in modelling as well. I often set up my own model shoots at home in my bedroom after I've been to the gym, setting my camera on a timer and getting myself into a suitable pose. The two hobbies complement each other well, and I hope that one day I can have a career that involves both.

·♥·♥·♥·♥·♥·

I still feel incredibly guilty about also being given the apprenticeship. It just doesn't feel right. As much as I *love* photography and it is a passion of mine, I also love being *in front* of the camera. The gym guy from college got me into working out and I've become massively confident with my body and I'm impressed with my progress. I go to the gym four times a week, so my body would definitely be something the magazine would be looking for as part of their 'Gym Freak' category. I wish I had applied for the *job* of a model rather than the *apprenticeship* of a photographer. It suddenly clicks with me that maybe I should phone Stacey Cheng and let her know I've changed my mind. But, I remember I've already signed a contract.

Shit.

This isn't what I want. I don't want to be an apprentice photographer anymore. I want to be a model.

Danny

I PACK MY CAR full of all the essential things I'll need to take to London with me, at least to get through the first couple of weeks. I can bring anything else I need back when I return home in a couple of weeks for the weekend. Dad carries one last box over to the car and places it in the gap that is left in the boot - it just about squeezes in.

"Is that everything?" Dad asks.

"Yeah," I say, "I think so."

I close the boot and lock the car before heading back indoors to spend a bit of time with Mum and Dad before I leave. It's 9am and I need to be in London by 2pm to meet the landlord of my studio flat. I don't know *who* they are,

I don't even know what they *look* like so I have no idea who to look out for.

"You ready?" Mum asks, already starting to get emotional.

I nod, trying not to let the tears push their way through and pour from my eyes. "Yeah." I can't think of anything else to say. As soon as Mum sees that I *am* ready to leave, the tears form and fall down her face.

Great, now I'm going to cry, too.

Tears drip down my face like rain drops down a window on a cold and wet day. I hug her tightly, just like I used to every morning before school when I was six years old. It feels like a forever goodbye, even though I know it isn't. Leaving home to live somewhere new *away* from my parents is scary. Mum and Dad will be on the other end of the phone, but they *won't* be around the corner when I need them.

I pull away from Mum's embrace and go over to give Dad a hug.

"Good luck, son," he says, as he reluctantly places his arms around my back.

I smile and tears fall even heavier than before. God, how I *love* my parents, despite the ups and downs we may have.

Minutes pass and I decide it is time for me to leave home. I give both my parents one final hug and then I walk out the front door and climb into my car. Mum and Dad stand at the door, waving as I reverse out of the driveway. Just before I set off, I put the passenger window down and shout "I love you!" to my parents. Mum blows me a kiss and Dad waves at me. I drive away, waving to my parents as I roll past the house and then that is it. I'm officially on my way to London!

·♥·♥·♥·♥·♥·

The traffic on the M3 is building up and I'm beginning to grow anxious about being late for the meeting with my new landlord. Everyone comes to a stand-still and I put my car in neutral and apply the handbrake. There seems to be no sign of movement. Blue flashing lights shine in my rearview mirror and I try to manoeuvre over to the left to make space for the vehicle to come through. Obviously there is an accident up ahead which is causing significant delays. I realise I'm only about two miles from a service station so I decide that when the traffic starts to move again, I'll swing by there and take a short break from driving. Sitting in traffic is going to tire me out.

Someone blasts their horn behind me. I look in my mirror and see a middle-aged man, looks about fifty, with a bushy beard sitting in a large 4x4 truck.

"Dick," I mutter.

The middle lane of the motorway starts to slowly move, so I reckon it's only a matter of time before my lane starts to move as well. I put my car into the first gear, preparing to move off. And just as I place my hand on the handbrake to release it, the cars in front of me begin to move forward. I head off, going no more than ten miles per hour, but the traffic starts to slow down again before coming to a complete stop for the second time on my journey.

"This is ridiculous," I say, scowling.

I look at the clock on my screen. It switches from 10:58 to 10:59 within seconds of me looking at it. I think I'll be okay for time, but that doesn't stop me from worrying. I wish I had got the train - I'd be able to bring my car up next time I'm back home.

The traffic starts moving again and before I know it, I'm approaching the service station. No one was moving very fast, and there was the odd time when we came to a stop, but now, as I enter the slip road up to the service station, I breathe a sigh of relief. Finally, I get to have a break from everything on the road and take a bit of time for myself.

·♥·♥·♥·♥·♥·

I sit down at a table in Greggs with a sausage roll and a hot chocolate. The buzz of travellers fills the service station - kids bouncing past the arcade games, the sound of hand dryers blasting from the toilets, beeping from the McDonalds machines, the chatter of families as they sit and take a break from their travels.

I sign into Facebook after texting Mum to let her know where I have stopped. Ellie has posted a photo from our afternoon out, with a status:

Today, my best friend in the entire world moves onto his next adventure. Danny, you are my absolute rock - thank you for everything! I wish you all the best with your apprenticeship and I cannot wait to hear all about it when you come home in a couple of weeks. Go and be awesome. Love you xxx.

I smile as I read her lovely words and I stare at the photo, zooming in on everyone's face, each grin lighting up my screen. I have such a wonderful group of friends and I'm going to miss them massively. Mum replies to my text message, telling me to be safe and to let her know when I arrive at the flat. I close the message and then head to the toilets, throwing my rubbish in the bin along the way.

Christ, it stinks in here.

Sitting back in my car, I switch on the engine and head back onto the motorway. Hopefully, the traffic won't be too bad now. I build up my speed, overtaking the traffic that is going incredibly slow for the motorway, and merging back into the correct lane. I love motorway driving, but I also *despise* it at the same time. I see a sign directing me towards London, which should only be about forty-five minutes away now.

·♥·♥·♥·♥·♥·

I arrive in London and head towards the street my flat is on. As I pull up outside, I notice a very smart looking Range Rover parked up opposite the main door, and a man dressed in a suit sitting inside. Is he the estate agent? I climb out of my car and lock it before wandering over to the flat. I linger for a few minutes before the man in the Range Rover approaches me.

"You must be Danny?" he asks.

I nod with a smile. "Yes." I offer my hand for a handshake, and he accepts.

"Hi Danny, I'm Andy. Shall we head inside?"

I follow Andy into the flat and I'm not surprised by what I'm presented with. There are two rooms: one large one which combines the kitchen, living room *and* bedroom, and then one smaller one which has a toilet and a shower. I shouldn't complain though, it's something to start me off with and it's somewhere to sleep.

"So, as you can see," Andy begins, "it isn't the *biggest* property. But, it's very homely and will do you just fine."

I don't reply and let Andy continue his speech. "The bathroom just comes with a toilet and a shower, but there is a communal bathroom downstairs which has a bath in it, should you wish to bathe."

I screw my face up. Share a bathroom with a bunch of strangers? No thank you. The building seems too small to have much communal space, but Andy explains that along with the bathroom, there is also a communal games room. Is this a block of studio flats or a hotel?

About an hour later, Andy hands me the keys and he leaves me alone to get settled in. I look around the flat myself to check everything out. The sofa pulls out into a bed, and it feels like the most uncomfortable thing to sleep on. But it'll have to do for now until I can get my own one.

I head downstairs to my car and start bringing the boxes of my belongings in, making about eight trips in total. As I stand in the middle of the main room, as I like to call it, I can't help but glare at all the boxes. There's so much stuff and so *little* space for it all. God help me, this is going to be a *long* afternoon.

Harry

"You can't just change your mind!" Stacey Cheng yells down the phone. "You've signed a contract!"

I compose myself. "I understand, Stacey. Really, I do. But in all honesty, I don't want to be a photographer; I want to be a model. I've got the confidence, I've got the body for one of your categories, I've got the attitude and I've got the work ethic. I'll work extremely hard for this gig if you just give me a *chance*."

I tell her that I have a portfolio of modelling I have done in the past, and I can send it to her via email for her to browse through. But, by her tutting and sighing, I already know she isn't at all interested.

"I'm sorry, Harry, but you can't just *change your mind.* There is a process we have to go through and I don't have the time for it!"

She is obviously not going to give in to my request, no matter how hard I push. But I am *determined* to make her void the contract.

"Please," I beg, "all I want is to follow my passion. As much as I love photography, it's not something I'm *so* passionate about that I want to make it my career. I feel like modelling is the more realistic route for me."

Stacey scoffs. "Fine, whatever." She hangs up.

I take a few deep breaths. I can't believe she's done this. Maybe going for a job at this magazine was a bad idea after all. I'm distracted by my overwhelming anxiety and frustration that I don't see the van going fifty miles-per-hour on the motorway, instead of the seventy that I'm going. It's too late. The last thing I remember is the loud, stomach-churning smash of my car hitting the rear end of the van.

·♥·♥·♥·♥·♥·

My eyelids flutter as I begin to rouse from my unconsciousness. The gentle beeping of machines around me and the sound of people chatting away, pushing trolleys, and footsteps on the floor fill my ears with dread.

"He's coming round," I hear someone say.

I open my eyes, ever so slightly, and I see my mum towering over me, her eyes full of fear but her mouth stretching into a smile of relief. It suddenly occurs to me that I'm in hospital. Why am I here?

"Mum?" I croak. My throat feels incredibly dry and itchy. I let out a gentle cough, but all that does is cause me chest pains.

"It's okay, darling," Mum says, soothingly. "I'm here."

Machines beep closely in my ear. I struggle to move, my entire body aches. I groan as pain shoots through my body, causing me extreme discomfort.

"Try not to move," Mum instructs me, "you've not long had major surgery."

I cough again, the chest pains returning. "Surgery? For what?"

I see tears form in Mum's eyes. She strokes my forehead, and sniffs. She's beginning to make me worried - more worried than I have been, and I demand that she answers me immediately.

"You were in a serious car crash on the M3," Mum tells me, "and you were trapped. You hit a van at *full speed*. The fire crew had to cut you out of the car. The paramedics told the nurses that your left leg was completely crushed."

My breathing grows heavier. Until Mum just mentioned it, I hadn't thought about my legs. Now, I try to look down at them. But excruciating pain shoots up my spine and to my neck. I groan.

"They had to amputate your leg." Mum bursts into tears. "I'm so, so sorry, my baby!"

I try not to panic, but having just realised that's the reason I have no feeling in my left leg, my breathing becomes even heavier and before long, my heart is pounding against my chest at what feels like a million miles per hour. The machines next to me scream for the nurses to rush into the room. They gather around me, trying to calm me down, giving me oxygen to help me through this panic attack.

Everything around me just becomes a blur. I've no idea what is happening now. My eyes close and that's the last thing I remember before my phone wakes me up from my sleep.

With all the strength I have, I reach over to pick up my phone and answer it. I slowly raise it to my ear, aches spreading through my arms and chest, and speak into it. My voice still sounds croaky.

"Blimey, you sound awful!" the lady on the other end says. It's Stacey. "I've emailed you a contract. It needs to be signed by the end of today."

"There's a bit of a problem with that," I say. "I'm in hospital. I was in a car crash and it's going to be at least a few days before I'm out of here."

"What?!"

Her tone tells me she's not best pleased about me crashing my car. But, to be honest, neither am I. "I'm sorry. But I can't model for you right now. Maybe not ever.

I had to have my leg amputated, so you probably don't want me now, anyway."

She goes quiet for a long moment, before responding. "I'm so sorry, Harry. You take all the time you need to recover. As a goodwill gesture, I'm going to keep your contract open for negotiation in three months' time."

"Three months? Wow, that is *so* good of you." I roll my eyes.

"Isn't it? Well, I'll let you recover and speak to you soon. Ta-ra!"

Bitch.

I thump my arm down on the bed, my phone dropping to the floor. I grunt as I realise I can't lean over to pick it up. Nobody is in the room, they must have all gone home. The faint rattle of trolleys in the corridors echoes through to my room, filling me with anxiety. I hate the fact I'm still in the hospital. All I want right now is my own bed, in my own room, where I can get some adequate rest. I look lift my head slightly to look down at where my leg once was. The amputation is below the knee so there is still a chance that I can have a prosthetic leg if I decide to have one.

The door swings open gently and my mum enters the room. "How are you feeling?"

I chuckle. "Living the dream."

Mum smiles. "Seriously, love. You really scared me earlier."

I let out a heavy sigh. "I just freaked out, that's all. First, I find out I'm in the hospital, and then you drop that *huge* bombshell on me. It all got too much."

"I'm sorry." Mum sits down in the seat next to my bed and holds my hand. "I thought it was best you knew sooner rather than later."

I shake my head. "You don't need to apologise. I'm just grateful to be alive."

I'm very lucky to be here. But, in spite of all that, even though *I* didn't die, my dream of being a model certainly has.

Harry

I LEFT THE HOSPITAL a week ago, and now I'm back home. Mum and Dad had transformed the dining room into a downstairs bedroom for me whilst I was in hospital. They moved all of my belongings downstairs and arranged the room in a way that was accessible for me whilst I'm in the wheelchair.

Even my uncle donated some of his time to help build a ramp for the front and back doors of the house, so it was easy for me to get in and out. I'm extremely grateful for everything they've all done. But, even with all their kindness, I still feel somewhat unhappy. This shouldn't be my life. This isn't what I had planned. I had all these hopes and dreams. I was going to be a model, or a photographer, and I was going to travel around the UK - maybe even the *world* - modelling or photographing for huge brands. And now, here I am in a dining room turned bedroom, sitting in a wheelchair with a leg and a half, unable to do a lot for myself. I can't walk, I can't go to the gym. I can't do anything!

"Would you like a cup of tea?" asks Mum.

I shake my head. "No thank you. I just want my bed."

I wheel myself over to my bed, running my hands along the tyres of my wheelchair as they turn. I hop out of my chair and into bed, pulling the covers right up to my neck. Although I can't see her, I can sense Mum lingering in the doorway.

"Please leave me alone," I mumble. "I just need some time to myself."

A moment later, the door closes gently. I hear Mum and Dad whispering outside my room. It's tricky to make out what they're saying, but a long moment after, I hear Mum weeping. This is all my fault. If I had been paying attention to the road, I wouldn't be in this mess right now. Mum wouldn't be upset, I wouldn't be crippled, and I would be in London ready to start my career as a model.

·•·♥·♥·♥·♥·

I wake up from an afternoon nap, unaware of how long I've been asleep for. I look down at my legs, staring at my amputated left side. My heart starts to race as I become overwhelmed with emotion. Tears trickle down my face again as I recall my car accident, my mind repeating the events and pushing them through me.

I couldn't see the van. It was going so slow, and I was going at the speed limit. If I had just paid a bit more attention, I could have slowed down or overtook it. Why am I so bloody stupid?

I roll over and lift myself into my wheelchair. Once I'm settled, I rub my forehead as a headache begins to brew. I wheel myself out of the room and head to the kitchen. Mum is digging through the cupboards and throwing tins in the bin.

"What are you doing?" I ask.

"Clearing out," says Mum. "How are you feeling?"

"Is there any paracetamol? I've got a headache coming on."

Mum opens the medicine cupboard and hands me a couple of pills and a bottle of water from the fridge. I swallow the pills and then wheel myself over to the patio doors where I stop and stare out of the window. The rain is hammering against the glass and spreading across the patio, creating a surface as slippery as an ice rink.

"The weather is disgusting," I say. "Is it meant to stop at any point?" I don't bother turning around to listen to Mum's reply.

"No." I hear her throw another tin in the bin. "It's been raining since lunchtime and isn't meant to stop until lunchtime tomorrow. So, no football for you." Mum chuckles, but I don't find myself joining in.

"I'm sorry," she says, realising I haven't reacted in the way she hoped I would. "It was just a little joke. Look, I'm going to create a GoFundMe page. People can donate money and we'll hopefully raise enough to fund a prosthetic leg for you."

I turn around. "Really?" My face lightens up at the thought of being able to walk again.

"I'm going to try my best."

Mum walks over to me and gives me a hug. I really need this. This is the boost I've needed since I woke up in the hospital.

Danny

My apprenticeship starts today, and I can't wait to get started. Stacey Cheng emailed me a timetable for my first week last night and I have a day in college on Thursday, but every other day is spent working with the magazine.

I clamber out of bed and stumble over to the kitchen in a tired state, pulling the fridge open and pouring myself a glass of cold orange juice. I slide two slices of bread into the toaster, push the switch down and wait for it to pop back up again. As I pull the curtains open, the sun beams through the window, heating the glass and reflecting straight into my eyes. I squint and close the curtains again to block the light.

I swing around and stare at my half empty flat. Since moving in, I've had time to buy paint for the walls, but I haven't had time to actually start decorating yet. That's going to be my evening and weekend job for this week. With my apprenticeship being 9 to 5, Monday to Friday, I should have plenty of time to get the main bulk of my flat decorated without it looking tacky. There also still isn't a lot of furniture in here, so I need to treat myself to a shopping trip once I've been paid.

Once I finish eating my breakfast, I head into the hallway. I decided to transform the small cupboard into a wardrobe so I can hide my clothes from guests and have somewhere to organise them. I pull out a nice blue and white striped collared shirt, and a pair of pale blue skinny jeans with rips in various places up both legs. As I begin to get dressed, my phone rings.

It's Mum.

"Hi, Mum," I answer.

"Hello, darling!" Mum beams. "Good luck for today. You're going to smash it!"

I chuckle. "It's only an introductory day. Nothing too exciting."

"No, but it's the start of something big for you. Just think about all the opportunities that could come your way after this."

"I know, but I'm not going to hold my breath over it. I just need to take it a day at a time."

Mum agrees with me and then proceeds to change the subject, asking me about the flat and whether I've had time to do anything with it yet. I explain that I've managed to buy paint to *start* decorating as soon as I can, but nothing has been done yet. I tell her all about my DIY wardrobe, and I even switch to FaceTime so that I can show her around. She said that she'll come and visit with Dad in a few weeks so they can see the flat in person, so I'll have to make sure it looks somewhat presentable by then.

"Anyway, I need to go," I say, "I've got to leave in ten minutes. I'll speak to you later, love you lots."

"Bye, love," Mum says, "I love you too." Mum blows a kiss down the phone and then ends the call.

I pull my jeans up and secure them with a belt, before gathering my things that I need for the day and stuffing them into my backpack. I slide my Vans shoes on, swipe my keys from the kitchen counter and then leave the flat. My first day travelling to work. This is *very* exciting.

·♥·♥·♥·♥·♥·

I arrive at the studio ten minutes before nine o'clock, showing my eagerness and my punctuality. Stacey Cheng greets me in the reception area and shows me up to the staff room where I can store my belongings in my own locker, and I've even been assigned my own mug. I didn't even think to bring one, so I'm glad they have plenty to go round.

"I'll introduce you to the team as we go round," says Stacey.

There's only a small group of people in the staff room, all chatting away to themselves. Stacey wanders over to them and interrupts their conversation to introduce them to me.

"Everyone," she says, "this is Danny, he's our new apprentice starting today in the photography studio."

"Hey, Danny," a blonde-haired lady says, "I'm Amy, one of the editorial assistants."

I smile at her just as a man with dark hair and a short, well-groomed beard greets me. "I'm Will, one of the lead photographers. I guess we'll be working together."

God almighty, he's gorgeous.

His kind, emerald, green eyes pierce my heart as it begins to pound against my chest. Where did he come from, and how is a creature as gorgeous as him gracing this planet?

"Shall we head down to the studio?" Stacey says, startling me and rousing me from my moment.

"Yes, sure," I respond with an eager grin.

I look back and my eyes are glued on Will. He looks like he's in his early thirties, but Christ, I would *have* him. But he must be straight - he's definitely straight. He looks the type to be a lady magnet, if he isn't in a relationship and would rather be having one-night stands. I'll have to do some digging, find out more about him. If I'm going to be working alongside him, I should make an effort to get to know him.

Stacey guides me into a large room on the third floor of the building, kitted out with lightboxes, a large white backdrop, and various other photographic equipment that must be used on a regular basis.

This is amazing.

"This is the studio which you'll be working in," Stacey explains. "As Will said just now, he is one of the lead photographers. We do have two others, but they aren't in today. You'll meet them on Wednesday, but their names are Becky and Clive."

"I'm looking forward to meeting them," I say.

"Obviously, you won't be working with everyone all the time," continues Stacey. "The lighting technicians usually go into their office-" Stacey points to a small office on the opposite side of the studio - "and leave the photographers and directors to it, unless there is a problem with the lighting. But we'll train you up as if you're left working on your own, you'll need to know how to rectify any *minor* issues with lighting. The major ones should always be left to the professionals."

I nod, not knowing what to say. "Understood." I think that was probably the best thing to say, showing that I acknowledge what she said, but not being sarcastic about the fact that it is common sense to leave major issues to the people who actually know what they're doing - and to do the job they've been hired for.

"Right," says Stacey, clapping her hands together, "I'm going to introduce you to the rest of the team in the company. Follow me."

Stacey leads me out of the studio, and we head back downstairs towards the reception area of the building. "This is Camilla, our Administrative Manager."

Camilla looks up from her computer screen and gives me a friendly smile. "Hello, nice to meet you."

I offer my hand for a handshake. "I'm Danny, lovely to meet you too." We exchange a quick handshake before Stacey ushers me through and into the back office to meet the rest of the administrative team. As nice as it is to meet everyone, I'd rather just get on with what I'm here to do. Introductions can be done as and when I come across people. This all feels too unnatural for me.

Now I've met everyone who works on the admin side of the company, Stacey insists she takes me to the publishing house across the car park. I'm hesitant, and I excuse myself for a toilet break. Stacey shows me where the toilets are and I go in, taking a few moments to myself and take a breather. It's almost like she doesn't want to quickly introduce me to the *job*, but rather just to the *people*. I'm not a fan of all this, I just want to get on with it.

I head out of the toilets and ask Stacey when my apprenticeship will actually begin. I've spent the last ninety minutes being dragged around a huge building meeting everyone. And, as nice as that is, it wasn't exactly my ideal first day I had planned out in my head this morning when I woke up. It's approaching 11:00am, and I haven't even been shown *any* equipment yet. If it doesn't happen today, I *pray* it happens tomorrow.

Harry

Mum's GoFundMe scheme worked, and we raised more than enough money to fund a prosthetic leg for me. My swelling has gone down a lot quicker than we all expected, and even the doctors are surprised by how quickly I seem to be recovering. I have a meeting tomorrow to have a prosthesis fitted to my size and then I can begin physio. I rang Stacey Cheng this morning to let her know that I would like to keep my place as a model for the magazine, and as soon as my physio has begun, I can start looking into properly starting to work there.

"Are you sure this is what you want?" Mum asks.

"I'm sure," I reply."

"I'm just worried about you maybe not being able to handle any hate comments that come your way."

I nod. "I know. But I'm a big boy now, Mum. I can handle a few dickheads on the internet if it means I get to be a model for my favourite gay magazine."

"Okay." Mum wraps her arms around my shoulders and plants a massive kiss on my stubbly cheek. Since my accident, I have fallen into a depressive state and haven't taken much care about my appearance. I shaved a few times, but I've mostly just let it grow because I can't be bothered to get rid of it all. I also haven't had a proper haircut. Maybe I should get one *before* I start modelling. But I've made a promise to myself that I'm going to look after myself better and this modelling gig is just what I need to get my head in the right place again.

·♥·♥·♥·♥·♥·

It's been three hours since my appointment, and I'm having a prosthetic leg fitted. The doctor said the process can take a few weeks, and it will take a few sessions of physiotherapy to get used to the prosthesis, but I'm confident that within three months, I'll be modelling for the *Rainbow Gazette*. Mum is delighted for me, Dad doesn't know yet - he's away on a business trip, but he'll be home next week. I'll break the news to him then. I'd rather tell him in person, anyway.

Mum and I sit on the sofa, enjoying a hot chocolate together and watching my favourite movie, *Mean Girls*.

"I'm really pleased with today," I say, before taking a sip from my mug.

"Me too," Mum replies, "it's such great progress, and I'm really looking forward to seeing you getting your life back on track."

I nod. "And the opportunity to model for the *Rainbow Gazette* is still active. I've texted Stacey Cheng to let her know that I could be working within three months."

"Don't get too ahead of yourself. We don't know how long the physio will take."

Deep down, I know that Mum is right. But I want to have something to look forward to. I *need* something to focus on and to motivate me to work as hard as I possibly can in my physio sessions.

Danny

I BUMP INTO WILL in the staff room as I make myself a hot chocolate, topping it with marshmallows. He slides past me and grabs a slice of bread, popping it into the toaster.

"Morning," he says, a flirty grin on his face.

I don't know how to react. I'm not sure how old he is, possibly late twenties, but would he *really* be flirting with *me*?

"Hey," I say. "You okay?"

"All the better for seeing you." He winks at me, and chuckles.

I roll my eyes and sigh. "Do you know when I'll be starting to get into the studio and getting hands on with the photography?"

"I think Stacey has booked you in for a training session with me today," he says, "but I will double check for you."

He walks over to the whiteboard on the other side of the staff room and checks the timetable for the day. "Yep! You're with me for the morning, and with Amy in the afternoon."

"Isn't Amy the editorial assistant?" I ask.

"Yep. She's going to show you what herself and the editorial team do."

I nod. "Right. And what will I be doing with you?"

Will chuckles and grabs his toast from the toaster. "What are you hoping for?"

I roll my eyes. "You need to stop with your terrible attempts at flirting, it's making me uncomfortable. In terms of photography, what will I be doing?"

Will sighs. "Sorry. You'll be shadowing me today; you won't really be getting hands on with anything. You'll observe what I do, take notes, develop your own style."

I sit down with my hot chocolate and Will joins me. I have to shuffle away slightly. His aftershave is so strong, he smells absolutely gorgeous. I look over at him and a nervous smile sneaks onto my face.

"You smell nice." I immediately regret what I just said. It was supposed to be a thought, not said out loud.

"Thanks," Will says. "Not too bad yourself."

The clock strikes 9am. "Time to go, I guess. Take me to your studio."

Will stands to attention and salutes me. "Yes, sir!"

I giggle and we head out of the staff room and down to the main studio. The director of the shoot is discussing the lighting they want for it, pointing at all the different lights that need to be used and the positions they need to be in. The lighting crew obey the director and start setting up for the first shoot of the day.

The director approaches Will and I, and hands us a brief. "These are the details of all of today's shoots. The first one is for a two-page spread. It's the love story of two men who were enemies at school - but really, it was just because they were in love."

I cringe. How can anyone fall in love with someone they hated?

The director turns to me. "I don't think we've met. I'm Kevin."

He offers his hand and I take it, shaking it firmly before letting go. "Danny."

"Pleasure to meet you. I assume you're shadowing Will today?"

"Yes, that's correct."

"Brilliant, you'll really get a feel for what goes on in here. Will is a *fantastic* photographer and teacher. Did you know he runs a photography club for teenagers in one of the local secondary schools?"

I look over at Will, offering him an impressed smile. "No, I didn't know that. That's amazing."

"It's mostly for the GCSE students who just want some extra sessions," Will explains. "I get some who don't study

GCSE Photography, or aren't even in their GCSE year yet, but they have a real talent."

"I bet. I expect high quality teaching from you then," I joke, winking at him.

Will chuckles. "High quality is just what I like to give."

"Right," Kevin pipes in, "I've got some office crap to do before Olly and Rhys arrive for their photoshoot. Enjoy, lads."

Kevin wanders away, leaving Will and I alone. He takes me to one side to talk to me privately.

"Is everything okay?" I ask.

"No," says Will. "I've been wanting to do this since I first laid my eyes on you."

I swallow saliva, my heart beating faster, and my face growing warmer. "What's that?"

Giving me no chance to back away, Will grabs my face and plants his lips on mine. I don't hesitate, and I allow him to kiss me as I kiss him back, embracing him for the short moment we have.

"Sorry," he says, as he pulls away and wipes his mouth. "That was unprofessional of me."

I look around the room. I don't think anybody saw; they're all too busy playing around with the studio setup to notice anything else going on.

"It's fine," I say. "Fancy getting a coffee together at lunch?"

"Is coffee a codeword for..."

I cut him off. "Coffee is a codeword for coffee. I'm asking if you want coffee. That's it. Maybe some cake if you're lucky." I wink at him. Now, cake *is* a codeword.

·♥·♥·♥·♥·♥·

This morning's photoshoot was great fun. Olly and Rhys are such a cute couple, and honestly, I regret my judgement before I met them. They're made for each other. I did feel a little bit jealous though since I don't have someone in my life that I can love the way they love each other. Maybe I should start the dating apps again and find my Mister Right on there.

I stand by the coffee machine in the staff room, making myself and Will a drink. As the coffee pod pours into the mug, I stick my fajita chicken wraps in the microwave, allowing them to heat up for a couple of minutes before tucking in. Will comes into the staff room and smiles at me. With the room being empty, we *know* that he can say and do anything, and nobody would know. I smile shyly and hand him a freshly made cup of coffee.

"So, what's all this about?" Will asks.

The microwave pings and I take my wraps out. "It's about what happened earlier."

Will froze. "Ah. Are you going to report me to Stacey?"

"No. No, quite the opposite actually." We sit down at the table, facing opposite each other. "I was actually going to suggest you could come round to mine. *Tonight*."

Will shifts in his seat. "Oh yeah? What for?"

"Maybe you could teach me a thing or two about photography. Show me that *high quality* you were bragging about this morning."

"Well, if that's what you want," Will says, "then you shall receive. What time?"

"Straight after we finish up here?"

"Excellent."

We eat our lunch together and finish our coffees before heading back down to the studio. This afternoon's photoshoot is for the fitness section of the magazine. Apparently, there's some gym freak coming in to model his toned body. Stacey told me he recently had his leg amputated, and whilst he awaits a prosthetic, he's going to be modelling in his wheelchair. I have to admit that it is pretty inspiring. I've also been told that he is a last-minute booking, he only decided this morning that he wanted to start modelling as soon as he possibly could, despite the fact he's in a wheelchair still.

"Right," Kevin calls out, "this afternoon's session is with a young man in a wheelchair. We need to make the studio as accessible as possible. He will be here in one hour."

I'm not really sure what to do to help, so I ask Will.

"If you could go down to the reception and ask for the ramp, that would be great," Will says. "We'll need it for the step that's just by the entrance to the studio."

I nod and head down to the reception. Camilla, who I met yesterday, is tapping away on her keyboard. As I approach her, she looks up and greets me with a friendly smile.

"Hey, Danny," she says, "what can I help you with?"

"Is it possible to have a ramp for Studio One?" I ask.

"Of course. Bear with me a second."

Camilla jumps out of her seat and unlocks a storage room that's located directly behind her. She disappears into the room and comes out a minute later with a small ramp. "Here you go." She hands it to me.

"Thank you very much," I say. "See you later."

I walk back to the studio and set the ramp up on the step, making sure it is secure and won't collapse under the weight of this bloke's wheelchair. Will comes over and double checks it for me. He says it is fine and carries on with what he was doing before.

I stand at the side, feeling like a bit of a plank, not really knowing what to do. Everyone else seems to be so on it, that there isn't really a place for me at the moment. So, I decide to go into the equipment office where the cameras are arranged on the shelf, in order of make and model. I pick up a Canon 1100d and hold it in my hands. This was my very first camera when I began getting into photography, but my grandparents upgraded me to a Canon 4000d, and I sold my 1100d. I attach an 18-55 millimetres lens to the camera body, and switch the camera on, fiddling around with the settings and the zoom on the lens.

"What are you doing?" a voice startles me.

My heart pounds against my chest as the anxiety of being caught red handed hits me like a slap across the face. I swing around and see Will standing in the doorway.

"Sorry," I say, "I was just having a play around with the camera. I had a Canon 1100d when I first started getting into photography."

"Very nice," he says, "now put it back. You're not to touch anything until instructed to."

"Sorry."

I disassemble the lens from the camera and put everything back where I found it. Will escorts me from the room and puts me in charge of greeting the model.

"He'll be here any second, so make sure you're polite, welcoming and sensitive," Will says.

"Of course," I reply. "I'll be on my best behaviour."

Will grunts and leaves me standing by the studio door. A few minutes later, the door opens and a man, around the same age as me, wheels into the room in his wheelchair and stops at the bottom of the ramp. I take a few steps over to him.

"Hi," I say, "I'm Danny." I offer him my hand for a handshake.

"Hey," he replies, taking my hand, an adoring smile on his face, "I'm Harry. Here for the modelling shoot."

He is gorgeous.

I clear my throat and call Kevin over. "This is Kevin, the director of the shoot."

"Hello," cheers Kevin, "you must be Harry."

"Yes, hi," says Harry.

Harry is so cute. Such an innocent face, and a deep, sexy voice.

I watch as Kevin pushes Harry's wheelchair over to the studio setup and talks him through everything. I'd love to get to know him.

Harry

Wow, I just met the most incredible boy. He is absolutely stunning, and I one hundred percent want to get to know him better. But the only issue is I don't know if he is interested in me. I'll have to do some digging, maybe ask some of the staff here what vibe they get from him.

I watch him assist the lead photographer set up the cameras and adjust the settings to make sure it works with the lighting and the environment. He looks so cute fiddling around with the camera. I'm so infatuated by him that I almost miss hearing Kevin speak to me.

"Sorry," I say, "I was in a world of my own."

"No problem," says Kevin, "it's only natural to be when you meet a cute young man such as Danny."

Crap. How does he know?

He giggles, clearly reading my face. "It's okay, you know. If you like him. I can tell him if you want me to." Kevin winks at me.

I smile, trying to hide my embarrassment, but I know I'm failing as I feel my face burning up. "I'm shy."

Kevin places a hand on my shoulder. "Do you like him?"

I don't really know how to answer that question. I only met Danny five minutes ago. Yes, I find him attractive, but I don't know the guy. Maybe I should ask Kevin to tell Danny I'm interested. Then, I *will* get to know him.

"Kind of," I reply. That's all I can think of. It doesn't feel right to say I *really* like him - not just yet, anyway.

Kevin hurries away, quick as a flash, and heads in Danny's direction. I turn around, not wanting to see what happens next. But, before I know it, someone taps on my shoulder. I turn my chair around and see Danny standing in front of me.

"Hey," I say.

"Hey," says Danny. He freezes. I'm about to ask him if he's okay, but then he starts speaking again. "We're ready for the photoshoot now."

His nervous tone of voice tells me that he definitely wanted to confront me about my feelings, but he was too shy to, so he ended up changing the subject. Danny swivels around on his heel, but then stops. I almost catch the back of his ankle with my front wheel.

"Woah," I say, "careful."

"Sorry," says Danny, turning back around to face me.

We stare at each other in silence. I want to say something. It's clear Danny wants to also say something. But neither of us do. Danny clears his throat and then guides me over to the photoshoot setup.

"Hello, Harry," says a bearded man. "I'm Will, the lead photographer. You've met Danny, he's assisting me today."

I smile and nod at Will. I notice the way he looks at Danny when he talks about him. Is there something going on between them? Surely there can't be, the bloke looks almost thirty. Danny must be my age.

I wheel myself into the centre of the setup and position myself in front of the brightly lit white backdrop. It's quite daunting being this side of the camera, I'm not used to it.

Will and Danny natter behind the camera, and a slight feeling of jealousy floods my heart. Danny's heart clearly lies with this dude and has no interest in me. How could I get this so wrong? Maybe coming here was a mistake. This should be a one-off, I'll tell Stacey on my way out that I don't want to do this again. Danny gave me the signal that he liked me five minutes ago, now he's giving me the signal he'd rather have an older man. I'm sick of the mixed messages I get from guys.

I'm roused from my internal anger when Will begins giving me directions on where to position myself and how to pose.

"I'd like you to hold your head in your hands," says Will, "and look sombre whilst you're doing so. We want to get an emotive feeling in this photo."

I do as he says, and the camera flashes, capturing the first photo of the shoot. I do a few shots in that pose, before I'm asked to change position.

"Now," says Will, "Danny is going to direct you." Will ushers Danny to the front. "Over to you, buddy."

Danny looks nervous. I can see the sweat dripping down his forehead in the light. It's obvious he's new to all this, doesn't have much experience directing models. But that's what this apprenticeship is for, and I'm willing to be patient with him - even *if* he did mess me around earlier.

"You're a gym freak, right?" Danny asks.

"I guess," I say, "I haven't been as much recently though."

"That's not a problem. My idea is that we show the readers that anything is possible, no matter your ability or disability. How would you feel about posing with your shirt off and showing off your muscles, letting the reader see that even if you're a wheelchair user, you can still keep up your fitness levels?"

I'm not sure about that. Is he just desperate to see me without my shirt on? Or is he genuinely wanting to capture what he just explained? I mentally slap my brain to stop myself from thinking stupidly. Of course he just wants to capture that feeling, he's just doing a job.

"Sure," I say.

I lift my shirt over my head, exposing my toned body to the entire room. Considering I just said I haven't been to the gym much recently, my body certainly doesn't show that. It looks like I've been every day!

"Wow," Danny mutters.

I try not to smirk, and I think nobody else heard him. "How do you want me?"

·♥·♥·♥·♥·♥·

The photoshoot ended about ten minutes ago, and now Will is showing me all the photos that were taken today. Some of them make me cringe - it's not natural to see myself in all these weird poses that I'd never normally do in a photo. As soon as the shirtless photos come up, I can spot Danny's mouth twitch, trying not to form a smile. There he goes again, the mixed signals.

"I think they work well," I say. "Hopefully the person writing the article will match what the photo is representing."

"Don't worry," Will says, "our writing and editorial teams are ace at their jobs. The article will do your photos justice."

"Brilliant."

Danny doesn't say anything. He's still looking at the photo on the screen - me, showing off my biceps, with a cocky 'gym-lad' look on my face.

"You can keep a copy if you like," I state, sarcastically.

"Sorry?" Danny says, whipping his head away from the screen, almost giving himself whiplash.

"You keep staring at that photo." I point to the computer screen.

A few people around me chuckle when they notice the photo that Danny was staring at. As Danny's cheeks turn bright red, I feel a little bit guilty for calling him out publicly like that. But, rather than backing down and apologising to him, I wheel my chair over to the door and leave the studio.

I hear the door swing open behind me as I move through the corridor, and a voice calling out, "Hey," when I don't stop. As someone runs in front of my wheelchair and stops, I come to an abrupt stop, almost toppling out of my chair.

"What are you doing?" I spit.

"More like what are *you* doing?" Danny hisses. "Calling me out like that in front of everyone? Who do you think you are?"

"Can you blame me? You've been giving me mixed signals ever since I arrived here. One minute you act like you're interested, the next minute you act like you're not. Then you perv and drool over one photo of me with my shirt off!"

"Oh come on, Harry! We've known each other for one afternoon, and you think I'm going to fall at your knees and beg you to date me just like that?"

I freeze. Does he like me?

"Wait," I say, "what are you saying?"

Danny shrugs. "I don't know. All I'm saying is, that stunt you pulled in there has blown any chance of you and I getting to know each other."

Danny walks away, before our argument can get any more heated. But I'm not finished yet, I still have something to say.

"That's it!" I yell. "Walk away. Go back to Will, he's clearly the one you're more interested in, anyway!"

Danny turns around and walks back over to me. "What are you talking about?"

"I see the way you look at each other." I've calmed down a bit now and my voice is softer. "You clearly like him and he clearly likes *you*."

"I don't *like* him," Danny claims. "We'll never date or anything like that. Probably just have a good time, that's all."

Wow, a player and a whore. What a man!

"Is that it?" I ask. "Only, the way you looked at me in there made me think you liked me. And the way you looked at *him* in there made me think you like *him*."

"That's it," says Danny, "not that it's your business, anyway."

I clear my throat. "Forget it, Danny. Like you said, there's no chance of you and I getting to know each other."

I wheel away and head to the lift to take me to the ground floor. I'm expecting Danny to come after me, tell me he's sorry, tell me he wants to get to know me, and then we leave together to go on a date. But that's clearly not going to happen - it's just in my imagination. Danny is stood by the staircase as the lift door closes.

Why do I always have such bad luck with men?

As I arrive on the ground floor, Stacey Cheng greets me at the lift. I exit the lift and we both head to the sofa area where we sit and have a chat.

"I don't think I can do this again," I say, "I had a huge fight with the apprentice, Danny."

"Oh?" Stacey seems surprised. "What about?"

"It's silly, really. We both clearly like each other, but he's such a player. I can't work around him."

Stacey's eyes divert over my shoulder. "Maybe you should let him explain?"

"Why should I?"

"Because he's right behind you."

Stacey gets up when Danny comes to sit down opposite me. "I'll leave you both to it."

I look over my shoulder to see if Stacey has gone - she has. "What do you want?"

"I came to say sorry," says Danny, "like *really* sorry. I didn't realise how much it would actually hurt you. I'm not seeking an instant relationship with anyone, I just want to play around and have some fun right now."

"I get it," I say, "but I wish you could have just been honest with me upstairs."

Danny nods. "I'm sorry about that too. Really, I am." He pauses. "Do you fancy grabbing a coffee in the cafe over the road when I finish?"

My face lights up. "Sure. When do you finish?"

"Half an hour. Did you want to stay down here and wait or did you want to leave and come back?"

"I'll wait." A smile stretches across my face. So much for not wanting to speak to him. He better not be messing me around again, and he better not bounce back and forth between Will and me.

Danny

I PACK THE LAST camera away in the equipment room before Will says I'm welcome to leave. Before I leave the studio to head to the staff room, Will stops me.

"Still on for tonight?" he asks.

I pause. Am I? I'm not really sure to be honest. I'm meeting Harry for a coffee, which could develop into a first proper date if we get along well - but, I'm not getting my hopes up. That's my negative trait - I get my hopes up too quickly about things and then it never goes my way.

"Sure," I say, although truthfully, I'm not sure at all.

Will smiles and ushers me to leave the studio. I head to the staff room and gather my things when I bump into Kevin.

"Hey, Danny," he cheers. "How did things go with Harry?"

"We're meeting for a coffee," I say, "we had a bit of a falling out but we've made up."

"Ay, that's fantastic. He's a nice lad and so are you, so I hope things do go well between you both."

"Yeah." I look down shyly. "Baby steps, though."

"Oh, absolutely, of course. Can't be rushing these things. Oh, before you go, can I have a very quick word?"

"Of course."

Kevin invites me to sit at the staff room table with him. I place my stuff on the chair next to me before I sit down opposite Kevin.

"I've noticed the way you and Will act around each other," he says.

"What do you mean?" I ask, trying to play dumb.

"One of the lighting assistants caught you kissing at the back of the studio yesterday. And you both act differently when you're with each other."

Crap. "What are you talking about?" I'm still determined to lie myself out of this, it's no one else's business.

"Look, I'm not judging. It's just that Will is known to be a bit of a player and sometimes a user. You shouldn't let him stand in the way of you and Harry building at least a friendship."

I clear my throat, feeling my face burning up. "I know you mean well, Kevin. But honestly, this is no one's business except mine and Will's. I have no interest in Will romantically, we're just having a bit of fun, that's all."

Kevin holds his hands up in defence. "Hey, like I said, I'm not judging and I know it's certainly none of my business. I just don't want the team to be facing the brunt of any awkwardness between you and Will if things don't go well. The last time we had a workplace romance, things didn't end well and both staff had to be let go."

"Well," I say, "like I said, I'm not interested in him romantically, so there certainly won't be a *workplace romance*."

I get up, grab my things, and hurry out of the staff room. The cheek of him, butting into something that has absolutely nothing to do with him. Maybe he is right, though. I should be careful around Will - he did seem *very* pushy on the day we first met. He's flirty with everyone, and I shouldn't be jealous of that. But, like Kevin said, he's known to be a player. I just hope he isn't messing me around.

As I head out of the building, I notice Harry lingering by the bus stop, flicking his phone screen up to his eye level every few seconds. I look at my watch - I'm ten minutes late. I hope he doesn't think I'm standing him up.

"Harry!" I call. When he looks over, I wave.

He waves back and smiles. I jog over so I don't leave him waiting around for me any longer, and we head towards the coffee shop across the road.

"Thought you weren't going to come," says Harry.

"Sorry," I say, "I got held up. Kevin wanted a chat."

"Anything interesting?"

"Not particularly. He hopes things go well today with us. And he wanted to chat about Will, too."

Harry stops his chair and looks up at me. "What about him?"

"It's fine, honestly. I have no interest in him, so you don't have any competition. I know we've only just met, but I'm truly interested in getting to know *you* more. No one else has my eyes."

A smile stretches across Harry's face - the cutest smile. He leads the way into the coffee shop and heads towards a table - not that he needed to, the coffee shop is empty, with the exception of a sweet elderly couple sitting by the window sipping on their drinks and nibbling on a Victoria Sponge slice each.

The cosy atmosphere makes the coffee shop feel extremely welcoming and homely. Lights hang fairly low, dimly lit, surrounded by a brown bowl-shaped lampshade. The brickwork on the walls makes the establishment feel urban and unique, whilst the canvas prints with coffee inspired quotes gives it that modern twist.

"What do you fancy?" I ask.

"A cappuccino please," says Harry. "Here." He hands me a £10 note.

"Absolutely not," I say, pushing the cash away. "It's my treat."

"No, no…" he waves the note at me… "it's *my* treat. I insist."

I don't want to argue with him, so I reluctantly take the cash from him and head over to the counter. The young girl working seems worlds away as she chews on gum and twirls the strand of hair hanging down by her ear. I ring the bell for service.

"Hi," she says, miserably. "What can I get for you?"

"Could I get a regular cappuccino, and a regular Americano, please?" I ask.

"Any vegan requirements?"

"Um…" I didn't think to ask Harry… "give me a sec. Harry!"

Harry looks over at me.

"Are you vegan?"

"No," he replies.

I turn to the girl at the counter. "No, just regular milk please."

She taps away on the screen. "Can I get you anything else?"

Blimey, does she want to sound anymore disinterested?

"Oh, yes please. Could I also get two slices of carrot cake, please?"

She taps away on the screen, and looks at me, as if her face is repeating her question from before.

"That's it, thank you."

She huffs. "That's eight pounds, and ninety-eight pence, please."

I hand her the £10 note and she gives me my change. I thank her and then head back over to the table.

"Well," I say, "I think she's definitely done for today, she's so miserable and *rude*."

Harry giggles. "You sound like my mum."

"What do you mean?"

"She always complains about rude customer service."

"And rightly so." I let out a gentle chuckle. "Anyway, did you enjoy today? Apart from our little blip, obviously."

Harry nods. "Yeah, I had a really great time. You're a fantastic photographer."

I smile. "Thank you. And you're a brilliant model."

We gaze at each other for a few seconds before the rude girl comes over to our table and places the tray down.

"Thank you," I say. She doesn't acknowledge me as she walks off.

"You didn't have to get cake as well," says Harry.

"I didn't," I say, "*you* did." I wink at him with a cheeky smile.

"Shush."

We both chuckle before taking a sip of our drinks and tucking into the carrot cake. It's a good cake, and my drink tastes delicious. Not worth the over-pricing, but it's delicious nonetheless.

I finish my slice of cake first and look at Harry who is still nibbling at the last quarter of his. We've sat in silence for a good five minutes now, and I'm nervous that we've already run out of things to talk about.

"So," I start, "how did you end up in a wheelchair? If you don't mind me asking."

"I was in a car accident," says Harry. "Funnily enough, I was on my way here for a meeting with Stacey Cheng."

"Oh, God, I'm so sorry."

"It's fine. I lost my leg, but I'm getting a prosthetic one soon. Should be a couple of weeks from now."

"Oh, that's amazing. It's good you haven't let your injury stand in the way of doing the things you want to do."

Harry nods. "Yeah. I mean, I was reluctant to come back to modelling at first. But my mum convinced me that I should. And to be honest, I just wanted to feel normal again after being cooped up in the house for weeks on end."

"I get that. You're on the mend, and that's the main thing."

Again, Harry and I sit in silence for a few moments, out of conversation. Is this how it's going to be? Running out of things to say to each other every so often and having to just sit in silence like we're doing an exam? I try to think of something to break the silence, but nothing comes to mind and no words escape my mouth. Then, my phone buzzes. Saved by the bell.

Hi, love. Your dad and I are coming to see you this weekend. Make sure your flat is nice and tidy ;) Love Mum x

I chuckle and look up at Harry. "Hey, sorry I'm gonna have to go. My parents are visiting this weekend, so I need to make sure my flat is ready. Fancy doing this again?"

"Yeah, sure," says Harry. "When are you thinking?"

"Sometime this week? I'm not totally sure yet. Wanna exchange numbers?"

Harry smiles at me. "That would be great." He passes me his phone so I can input my number into his contacts list. I text myself from his phone and then save his number to my phone before handing his phone back.

"Sorted. I really enjoyed today."

"Yeah. Me too."

"See you next time!"

I skip out of the coffee shop and head to my car that's sat in the car park on the opposite side of the road. Once I'm sitting in the driver's seat, I take a few moments to gather my excitement. Harry is the *nicest* guy ever, and I'm *so* glad we went on that date. I just hope Will doesn't ruin things for me.

·♥·♥·♥·♥·♥·

I arrive back at my flat and throw myself onto the sofa, resting my legs after a long day of standing around and walking back and forth. Then, I hear a gentle knock on the door. I huff, struggling off the sofa, and open the door where I'm greeted by Will. He's holding a bottle of cheap white wine.

"Hey, buddy," says Will, inviting himself in. "I brought wine!"

Before I even get a chance to say anything, Will has already made himself at home on the sofa. I click the door shut and join him, trying to keep a bit of a distance.

"Look," I say, "I'm really tired."

Will places his forefinger over my lips, hushing me. "Then I can wake you up." He winks. As he leans in for a kiss, my mind wanders back to Harry. But the desire for Will takes over. I allow him to kiss me, and before I know it, I'm kissing him back.

Harry

THE TRAIN ARRIVES AT my local station, and I exit it before making my way through the station and scanning my ticket to let me through the gates. A bus stop is two minutes up the road so I make my way over to it and await the arrival of the number nine bus. Ten minutes later, the bus arrives and I begin my journey back home.

I thank the bus driver as he lowers the ramp, and I wheel myself off the large vehicle and make my way down the road towards my house. I'm completely smitten with Danny. I can't put my finger on what it is about him, but there is just *something* that I've clicked with. There is definitely a gentle flame flickering between us, and I'm excited to see how it develops.

"Hi, love!" Mum calls from the kitchen as I close the front door. "How was the photoshoot?"

"It was really good," I reply, entering the kitchen and setting myself at the table. "Should be in next month's publication."

"Fantastic news! Why are you so late?" A cheeky smirk on Mum's face tells me exactly what she's thinking. "Who is he?"

My face warms up. "I don't want to say, not yet."

"Why not?"

"I want to make sure things are going somewhere first."

Mum sits down next to me at the table and takes hold of my hands, cupping them in hers. It's always nice when Mum does this; it makes me feel safe and loved. She looks me in the eyes and a warm, gentle smile stretches across her face.

"You make me so proud," she says, "and whoever this guy is, he's lucky to have met you. Are you going to be seeing each other again?"

I shrug. "I'm not sure. He lives in London now, I'm still down here. The distance will be a struggle."

"Long distance relationships work. And even if it doesn't, you two can still be good friends, surely?"

"I guess. I just don't want to get my hopes up. But, Mum, I really like him."

Mum ruffles my hair adoringly. "Then, you'll get your arse in gear and make some effort to go up to London to see him every weekend."

"*Every* weekend?"

"Well, yeah. If you want to make something work."

"Mum, I only met the guy this afternoon. It'll be weeks, maybe months before we know for sure where things are going."

"But you should still make the effort. I assume you've exchanged numbers?"

"Yeah, but-"

"There we go then. You've got a way of contacting him. Love, I just want you to be happy."

I nod my head. Mum's heart is in the right place, but she's making this a huge deal when it's still early days. Danny might not even want more than a second date. That's the problem with dating these days - you never know how someone feels, there's too many fake, toxic people around. I try to avoid dating apps for this very reason, although the fact I have an active account on one at the moment shows that maybe I don't think they're all *that* bad.

Mum places a tupperware in the microwave, and sets it down in front of me - the shepherd's pie she made last week. Although it's almost 9pm, and I'm not overly hungry now, I tuck into it just so I don't go to bed on an empty stomach. Once I've finished, I head into my bedroom and begin to undress, ready for bed. It's been a long day, so an early night is just what I need. As I snuggle into bed, I close my eyes and think about Danny, wishing he was here with me, cuddling and reminiscing about our date. Before I know it, I drift off to sleep, dreaming about how good things could be with Danny.

·♥·♥·♥·♥·♥·

I wake up at the crack of dawn as my alarm rouses me from my sleep. As my eyes flicker open, my wheelchair comes into focus. I frown and let out a sad sigh. I'm sick of using the wheelchair, I just want to be able to walk again. Thankfully, I get my prosthetic leg in a couple of weeks, and then I can start my physio to learn how to walk with it. Until then, I guess I'm stuck with that bloody thing.

I reach over and grab my phone from the bedside table. My facial recognition function unlocks my phone, and I'm welcomed with a text from Danny.

Good morning, mister x

A kiss! He sent a kiss with his text! I type out a reply and sign it off, also with a kiss, and then head onto my social media.

Breaking news: Gay couple from North Hampshire beaten to death in homophobic attack.

It feels like my heart has stopped beating as I read the headline over and over again. Why does hate crime *still* exist? I worry for my safety as I realise that my face will be plastered all over the next issue of *Rainbow Gazette*, and my palms begin to sweat. A tear trickles down my face as I look at the photo that accompanies the article - the couple who were killed were in their late twenties, and they look so happy together in the photo. And some cruel, disgusting bastards have taken that away from them. It scares me to think that this could happen to me at any point just being out in the streets, holding hands with the person I love.

The temptation to contact Stacey Cheng and withdraw from being in the magazine overrides every other emotion I'm feeling right now. I don't want to put myself at risk of being another helpless victim of a homophobic attack. But I take a moment to breathe. Why should I hide away? Why should I feel *ashamed* of who I am? Nothing is going to change the way these mindless, heartless, sick and twisted individuals think, but hiding away and staying invisible is going to let them win.

No, I decide. I'm going to stay in the magazine, and I'm not even going to change a single word of the article I helped write to go alongside the images. I can't let this news story put my head in a different perspective - I should be *proud* of who I am and how far I've come. But things need to change. *People* need to change.

I roll out of bed and lift myself into my wheelchair. As I enter the kitchen to make myself a bowl of cereal, Mum notices my glum look. I don't say a word as I take the box of Coco Pops from the kitchen counter and grab a bowl from the lower cupboard. I place them both onto my lap and wheel myself over to the table, where I set the bowl down and pour the cereal in.

"Is everything okay?" asks Mum.

"Fine," I mumble.

"Are you sure?"

I take the milk from the fridge. "Yes."

Mum sits down at the table with me and stops me from pouring the milk into my bowl of cereal. "I don't believe you. What's the matter?"

I huff. "I woke up to a headline on Facebook. A gay couple were beaten to death last night in North Hampshire."

Mum's face drops, and turns from a look of worry to a look of complete despair and sympathy. "Oh, love. Did you know them?"

I shake my head. "No, no. But...but it puts things into perspective, doesn't it?"

"What do you mean?"

"People like me can't even walk down the street without being hurt. Lowlifes shouting hurtful, ignorant words; the little bastards attacking gay people for *who they love!*"

Mum comes round from the other side of the table and holds me in a tight embrace as I break down, worried about what could happen to me - or what could happen to Danny. I gently push Mum away and look at her, directly in the eyes.

"I'm just scared," I say, "of what could happen to me. What if, one day, I end up like those two blokes? What if doing this magazine was a bad idea and it draws hateful attention towards me?"

Mum strokes my hair. "You will be *okay*. I won't let anything bad happen to you. Let people say what they want, they're just jealous and they have *nothing* better to do than spread hate because they're insecure about themselves."

I nod. "I guess you're right."

But for some reason, I'm not confident. Words have a deeper effect when they're targeted at you for who you are.

Danny

THINGS BETWEEN WILL AND I are slightly awkward here at the studio. Last night was amazing; *he* was amazing. But, I regret it. I want to build something special with Harry, and I just know my fling with Will is going to get in the way - especially after I told Harry that there wasn't anything between Will and I.

"Hey," says Will, "are you okay?"

I grunt a "Yes," and then carry on with what I was doing before he interrupted me. But, he doesn't leave. Instead, he sits down next to me.

"Was last night okay? I mean, did you enjoy it?"

I sigh. "*Yes*, I enjoyed it. But it didn't mean anything."

Will stretches his arm around my shoulders. "What do you mean? Of course it meant something."

"No, it didn't." I shake my head. "Don't you understand what I'm saying? It was a mistake, it shouldn't have happened."

Will clears his throat. "Is this something to do with that Harry guy?"

I shoot him a piercing gaze. "What?"

"Is there something you're not telling me?"

"There's nothing *to* tell you. It's none of your business."

"Oh, don't be like that. If you like him, then go for it. But, in the meantime, we can still have a little fun, right?"

"No."

Will huffs. "Suit yourself." He stands up and walks away.

I'm tempted to report him to HR. Although I enjoyed last night, I just don't want anything to happen again. And if Will carries on, I might have a case against him.

·♥·♥·♥·♥·♥·

It's lunchtime, and I'm sitting in the staff room tucking into my corned beef sandwich when Stacey approaches me. I smile and place my sandwich down on top of the clingfilm I had wrapped it in.

"Hey," I say.

"Can I have a word?" Stacey asks.

"Sure."

Stacey sits down on the chair opposite me and pulls a folder out of her bag. "I've just been speaking to Will."

I stare at her. "Okay?"

"He's disclosed that there is some kind of relationship between the pair of you and I just need to discuss it to make sure there are going to be no implications in the workplace."

I chuckle. "I can assure you there is *no* relationship between Will and I. We spent last night together and that's it. Too much information, I know, but I'd rather be up front with you and tell you the *actual* truth rather than his fantasy version."

Stacey looks confused. "He told me you were going on dates. Is that not correct then?"

"I can confirm that is definitely *incorrect*. He's jealous because I don't want anything else to do with him. We work together, we're colleagues, and that's how I want it to stay."

"Hmm, okay. I'll speak with Will."

"Yeah, please do."

Stacey jumps up from the table and grabs a custard cream from the biscuit tin on her way out of the staff room. I'm too pissed off to finish my lunch - I don't understand why Will is doing this. Is he jealous? Is he a creep? I should have listened to Kevin when he warned me about Will being a player. Because not only is he a player, but he's also a bit of a bastard.

·♥·♥·♥·♥·♥·

It's the end of the day, and as I head to my car, Will rushes over to me from his motorbike. I try my best to ignore him, but as he invades my personal space, I can't help but snap at him.

"Back off!" I yell. "Why can't you just leave me alone?"

"Hey, I just want to talk," says Will. "I was hoping we could have a repeat of last night."

I scoff. "Are you joking? Last night was a *mistake*! I told you this morning, I don't want anything to do with you in that way. We work together and that is *all*!"

"Stacey spoke with me earlier."

"Oh, did she? Did she warn you to stop telling lies about me? About us?"

"No, she just said we both need to make sure we're professional about this."

"I'm trying to be. You're the one who keeps...*harassing* me!"

"Harassing you? I just want some fun."

"Well, I don't. Not with you, anyway. Goodbye, Will."

I climb into my car and glare at Will with a frustrated gaze before shooting off through the car park. I spot him in my rear view mirror climbing onto his motorbike and pulling the helmet over his head. I exit the car park and head down the road.

Traffic is building up along the main road, and I get caught up in a long queue of cars. I put the car into neutral and apply the handbrake, letting out a sigh of frustration as the traffic is showing no sign of moving anytime soon. In my right wing mirror, I spot Will on his motorbike approaching up the side. He slows down and stops next to my car, signalling for me to lower my window. I ignore him, and keep my eyes on the road ahead, waiting for the cars to start moving again. Clearly annoyed with this, Will taps on my window and doesn't stop. In anger, I lower my window and yell at him to go away. As I start to bring the window up again, Will sticks his hand in between the window and the roof, prompting me to stop so not to hurt him,

"Will you just leave me alone?" I shout. "You're a creep!"

"You weren't saying that last night," Will laughs.

"How many bloody times do I have to tell you? Last night was a mistake and it should not have happened! Carry on and I'm reporting you to HR for harassment and stalking in *and* out of the workplace."

I close my window and begin to slowly move my car forward as the cars in front in forwards a few metres. But, then I'm brought to a stop again. When Will stops his bike right next to my car again, I make a decision to email HR when I get home to arrange a meeting with them. If I want to get through my apprenticeship comfortably, then I need to get something put in place regarding Will. And if I want to see where things go with Harry, then I need to make sure that Will won't be able to do anything to stand in my way.

·♥·♥·♥·♥·♥·

I arrive home an hour later after discovering the traffic was due to a hit and run, holding everyone up while the emergency services did their work. I throw my bag on the floor, place my keys on the sideboard, and kick my shoes off before going to lay in my bed for five minutes. It's been a long day and I need to de-stress before even thinking about making myself some dinner. Just as I close my eyes to rest them, my phone pings.

Hi love, hope you haven't forgotten we're coming up to see you this weekend. Can't wait to see you, I've really missed you. Love Mum xxx

Balls. I forgot Mum and Dad are coming up this weekend. I look around my flat and see the mess that Will and I made last night. Pizza boxes, bottles of cola, his bottle of cheap wine. I groan as I realise that it's going to take me a while to make the flat spotless from top to bottom. I roll out of my bed and start picking up the boxes and piling them up on the kitchen counter. They can go in the recycling bin tomorrow when I leave for work. The bottles can go in the bottle bank in the community centre car park that's across the road, so I put those in a bag so it's easier for me to carry over.

I open the fridge and pull out a microwavable chicken tikka masala. Just as I put it in the microwave, my phone pings again.

Hey, hope all was okay today. Missed you. I'm thinking about coming up to London next week - fancy a proper date? Harry xx

I smile adoringly as I read the end of his message - the two kisses. Something about receiving kisses in a message from someone I really like just gets those butterflies in my stomach fluttering around like they've never done before.

Work was so stressful today but it's a long story - definitely one for another time! That would be great, let me know what day and time. I can come pick you up from the train station if you like? Xx

As soon as I hit send, I knew I made a stupid mistake with that last part. How can I pick him up? My car is tiny and won't fit his chair in! I'm such an idiot.

That would be great. Just one question...what car do you have? Xx

I chuckle at Harry's reply. Obviously, my little Nissan Micra is not going to fit his wheelchair in, so I reply to him and tell him I will pay for his taxi.

No, no. You're not to do that. You can pay for lunch ;)
Deal.

The microwave pings and I take my curry out, placing it down on the kitchen counter whilst I make myself a drink. I sit down on the sofa and tuck into my dinner, watching the television as I savour every mouthful of the curry.

There's a knock at the door. I place my curry down on the arm of the sofa and head to the front door to open it. It's Will. I grunt and try to shut the door on him but his foot blocks the way.

"I want to talk to you," he says.

"Go away, Will!" I shout.

"No, not until you've heard what I've got to say."

Part 2

Will

"We have no choice but to let you go," says Stacey.

I lurch forward. "What? Why?"

"You're being a pest towards other members of staff. You're making everyone feel uncomfortable."

I scoff. "Is this something to do with Danny?"

Stacey nods. "Yes. He's told me everything, and honestly, I believe him. His formal statement to HR was the last straw. I'm sorry Will, but you're fired with immediate effect."

I storm out of Stacey's office with a face like thunder, and head towards the studio. I know for a fact Danny is in there, and I'm going to give him what for. As I enter the studio, door swinging open violently, everyone looks in my direction.

"Woah, where's the fire?" Kevin laughs.

"Piss off, Kevin," I growl, "where's Danny?"

"In the equipment office. Why, what-"

I walk away from him before he can finish his sentence. "Oi, snake!"

Danny turns around and looks at me, immediate fear written all over his face. "What?"

I stop in front of him, my face still a picture of anger. "*You've* just lost me my job!"

"Good!" Danny hisses. "You're a sex pest, and you haven't left me alone ever since we spent that night together. You deserve everything coming to you."

I hold back the temptation to slap him. He's made me so angry, and all because I just wanted to have a little bit of fun. He's going to regret it, that's for sure.

"So," I say, smugly, "how's your boyfriend?"

"He's not my boyfriend...yet," Danny grumbles. "Anyway, it's none of your business."

"But you want him to be."

"Maybe. But, again, it's none of your business. Now leave me alone before I report you to HR for a *second* time."

"You're going to regret this."

Like a bull in a china shop, I pace out of the studio and head towards the staff room to grab my belongings, ignoring everyone I walk past. Getting a new job is going to be difficult now that Danny has made those allegations. Stacey certainly won't be giving me a good reference, that's for sure.

·♥·♥·♥·♥·♥·

As the sky turns a beautiful shade of orange and yellow, I sit on my balcony watching the sun go down, the world continuing to function as normal, while it feels like mine is falling apart. Maybe I *did* go too far with Danny, but he didn't need to lose me my job. That job was my life, and now I have nothing.

My phone vibrates in my pocket so I fish it out, opening the message that I've received. As soon as I see it's from Stacey, I grunt, dreading what she's going to say to me now.

Danny has agreed to a mediation meeting, on the condition that you take it seriously. You're an asset to the company and we would hate to see you go. I'm revoking your sacking, but you will be temporarily suspended until further notice. I'm going to formally put all the details in an email and I will also give you a call in the morning. Stacey.

This is something, I guess. At least I still have a chance of keeping my job, even if it does take a few weeks to get back into action. Without responding, I tuck my phone back into my pocket and I lean back in the plastic chair, can of beer in one hand, and watch the sun fall from the sky behind the trees in the not-too-far distance.

As I sit here, witnessing the townspeople go about their evening duties, traffic lingering on the roads, and young kids playing in the park just across the road from my block of flats, I hear my buzzer ring. I struggle out of my chair and I head indoors to answer it.

"Hello?" I say.

"It's me," a familiar voice says in response. "Can we talk?"

I press the button to open the main door and leave my front door on its latch so Danny can come in. Nervously, I sit down on my sofa and take a few deep breaths whilst Danny climbs the three flights of stairs to reach my flat. I hear the front door click shut, and the presence of another human in my flat stands in the doorway to my sitting room.

"Hey," says Danny.

"Hi," I reply. "What do you want?"

"I just came to say sorry. I reported you to HR, hoping you'd at least get a strong talking to and maybe a temporary suspension. Honestly, I didn't mean for you to lose your job."

"Well, Stacey has revoked my sacking and has instead reduced it to a temporary suspension because you've agreed to a mediation meeting."

Danny nods. "Well, yeah. I guess we *should* talk about it and come to some sort of solution. But, I decided to come round tonight so we can talk, just the two of us, without the intervention of someone else too. I feel like maybe we can sort it out together, just by explaining both sides of the story."

Part of me sees where he's coming from. Another part of me wants to kick him out of my flat. How *dare* he come round here and start patronising me!

"Fine," I say, "let's talk."

I invite Danny to sit down next to me on the sofa, and he cautiously agrees. Neither of us say anything and it feels very awkward. I thought Danny would be the first to say something, but I guess he's thinking the same as me and hoping that *I'd* be the one to start.

I sigh. "Look, I'm sorry too. I didn't mean to make you uncomfortable. I just...I just felt like we had a connection, and then Harry came along and I got a bit jealous and tried to get you to like me more than you liked him."

"That's not the way to go about it," Danny explains. "You could have been upfront about your feelings, you didn't have to become a sex pest. There's no excuse for that."

I frown, genuinely feeling a little bit guilty about the way I've made Danny feel. "I'm sorry."

"Please...just don't do it again."

Danny stands up to leave. He turns around just before exiting the sitting room and looks back at me. "See you tomorrow?"

I nod. "Yeah. What time is the meeting?"

"Ten o'clock, sharp."

"I'll be there. And Danny..."

Danny turns back around again.

"I am sorry, I mean it."

He leaves my flat and once again, I'm alone. All I want is a man. I'm single, lonely and depressed. Danny brought a tiny bit of happiness to my life for the short while that we spent time together that one night, but now, I'm unhappy again.

And it's all my fault.

Danny

I LEFT WILL'S FLAT an hour ago and now I'm back in my own one, staring out of the window that sits just above my bed. The full moon shines brightly, like a big lamp in the sky, filling my flat with enough light that I don't even need my main lights on.

I look up to the stars, thinking about how I've got into this mess. I do like Will; really, I do. But, not anymore than just a friend. If this meeting goes well tomorrow, then maybe we can remain good friends and professional colleagues at work. But, if not, then I guess that's the end of the line for him. I certainly don't want to be working alongside someone who is going to be pestering me constantly for attention.

My phone buzzes. I turn the screen on, squinting at how bright it is, and read the message that has just come through to me.

Hope everything is okay. Haven't heard from you. Harry x

I smile, finding it adorable that he's been thinking about me. I type out my reply and hit the send button. At the moment, I don't think it's a good idea to explain the whole situation to him just in case he becomes insecure again. Things are going well, and I don't want this whole Will situation to get in the way.

Drawing the curtains, I settle down for the evening and switch on my bedside lamp. It's only 8pm, but I feel drained. And I haven't even been that busy today. It was a slow day at work today as there weren't many shoots booked in, so for me, it was a case of sitting in the editorial room and shadowing one of the girls who edits the photos that we shoot. She was absolutely amazing at what she does, and I hope that I can spend maybe a couple of hours a week in the editorial room to work on editing some photos, especially when we have days like today.

·♥·♥·♥·♥·♥·

I wake up before my alarm even goes off. As my eyes creep open, my room is filled with the gentle sunrise. I lay still for a few minutes to bring myself round to my surroundings. Tiredness takes over my entire body and before I know it, I'm drifting off back to sleep.

Jolting awake, I realise the time - 8:45.a.m.

Crap.

I jump out of bed and throw some clothes on. Today, I don't care what I look like - I'm going to be *very* late for work. I quickly brush my teeth, grab a Coco Pops bar from the cupboard, swipe my car keys from the side table in the hallway, and race out to my car. As I pull away, I realise I've forgotten my lunch. But, it's too late. I'll just have to go over to the coffee shop across the road from the studio during my lunch break to grab some food.

It's 9:20.a.m. when I arrive at work. My hands-free in the car has stopped working too, so I couldn't even contact Stacey to let her know. I rush into the reception area, sign in, and then hurry up to the staff room where I see Stacey angrily writing in her notebook.

"Morning," I say, out of breath. "I'm so sorry I'm late."

"Lateness isn't tolerated here. That's one strike on your name," Stacey snaps.

"Like I said, I'm really sorry. I'm usually so punctual, I think I was just so-"

Stacey holds her hand up and interrupts me. "I don't want to hear it. Go put your things away and then head to the editorial room. You're in there again this morning."

"Great!"

As I head back into the staff room after locking my coat in my locker, I turn to Stacey, noting that she's still looking rather flustered, like there's something serious going on that I don't know about.

"Are you okay?" I ask, politely.

"Danny," she says, "I don't have time for this. I've got enough going on with this situation between you and Will. I don't need you making my work any more stressful."

"Excuse me? What have I done?"

"You're late and made no effort to contact me, you walk in and act as if nothing has happened, and then I get a letter on my desk this morning telling me that the company just doesn't have the right funds anymore!"

I'm taken aback by what Stacey has just said - and the way she snapped at me. What did she mean 'the company doesn't have the right funds?' Are we going under? Is my apprenticeship at risk? Stacey can clearly see the look of anxiety on my face.

"Don't worry," she says, "you're safe. You're on a low wage so we can afford to keep you. It's the more senior staff who should be worried about their jobs."

"Like...Will?"

Stacey huffs. "Yes, Will could be one of them. Why?"

"No particular reason. I just don't want you to make any hasty decisions about him, we seemed to be able to actually talk about the situation last night."

"Oh, good. Sorted it?"

"Kind of. A mediation meeting would still be good though, so we can sort out our professional relationship.

Our private ones should be something to sort...privately. You know?"

"Yes. Now, go on. You've got work to do and I've got to sieve through all this paperwork and make some crucial decisions about the company. I'm not to be disturbed."

"Of course, sorry."

I rush out of the staff room and head to the editorial room where I'm greeted by the lady I was shadowing yesterday, Helen. She's set up a laptop next to her desk for me to use so I can get some hands-on editorial experience today, and she talks me through all the functions of the photo editing software.

"Do you think you'll be okay to work independently?" Helen asks. "I have an important meeting in half an hour so I won't be here for most of the morning."

"Yeah, I'm sure I'll be fine," I say, "but if I need anything, I can just ask someone else in the office, can't I?"

Helen nods. "Yeah. But, they'll be extremely busy putting the magazine together so it is highly unlikely that they will actually have the time to come over and give you some support in your training. See how you get on and if you do struggle, find something else to make yourself useful and when I'm back from my meeting, we can go through it together."

I give Helen a friendly smile. "Okay, thank you."

She sits at her computer and starts tapping away on her keyboard whilst I'm tasked with editing the photos from yesterday's shoot. An elderly transgender woman came in and told her story about how she used to be a soldier back in World War II. It wasn't what she wanted to do, but back then, because she was still considered a man by society, she had no choice. It wasn't until five years ago that she finally became her true self - Penelope. She was a lovely woman, and it was wonderful to hear that her family accepts her for who she is.

I open one of the images and stare at it for a few moments. The way Penelope poses, the way she oozes in confidence. She's an inspiration. I'm not one for making major changes to portrait photos, it doesn't feel ethical. I like to just retouch colours and lighting, I never make any changes to someone's appearance unless they request it such as spot removal. Penelope never requested any of her wrinkles being removed, so I leave them where they are. She deserves to have people see her and admire her for who she truly is.

·♥·♥·♥·♥·♥·

The clock strikes ten o'clock, and I sit in the meeting room anxiously waiting for Will to arrive. Our mediation meeting is due to start, and he's running late. A member of HR is sitting to my left, looking through a clipboard full of paper which I assume are notes about the situation.

I lean back in my seat just as there is a gentle knock on the door before it slowly opens. I sit up and watch Will walk in and approach the seat across from me.

"Sorry I'm late," he says.

The meeting lasts about an hour, and I'm satisfied with the outcome. Will has agreed to keep our relationship purely professional and he won't make any more advances towards me. I agreed that I wouldn't mention anything about my growing relationship with Harry around him so as not to appear as though I'm rubbing his face in it. When HR are happy with the way the meeting has gone, they let us go.

On my lunch break, I head to the coffee shop over the road and sit at the same table that Harry and I sat on when we had our first date. I order a regular hot chocolate, a ham and cheese toastie, and a slice of carrot cake. When I sit down, I pull my phone out of my pocket and text Harry.

Hey, any idea when you're coming to London next week? Xx

I take a bite of my toastie just as Harry replies.

Yes, I'll be coming up on Wednesday for another photoshoot, so we could always go out again afterwards. Xx

I smile and type out a reply. *That would be lovely. How about a proper restaurant date this time? Don't worry about booking a hotel for the night either, you can stay at mine. Xx*

Just as I press send, I cringe at my offer of letting him stay at my flat. We barely know each other, why would he want to stay at my flat?

That would be great, thank you. Xx

Thank God he didn't freak out. I finish my lunch and head back over to the studio.

Harry

The bus takes me to a stop that's about ten minutes from the photography studio. It's annoying that there aren't any buses that go directly there as it would be so much more convenient for me. Like I always do, I thank the bus driver and then head in the direction I need to go so I'm not late for my photoshoot.

As I arrive at the studio, the receptionist greets me with a friendly smile and I sign myself in. Then, I make my way up to the photography studio where I know Danny is waiting for me. He told me that Will was suspended earlier last week, but after an investigation and a successful mediation session, he's returning to work next week. I don't really like Will, he seems a bit of a sleze bag to me.

But, I'm here to do a job and so is he, so I will tolerate him professionally.

The lift stops on the first floor and I exit, making my way towards the studio. I see the door open and watch as Danny approaches me.

"Oh, hey!" he says. "We're almost ready."

"How did you know I was up here?" I ask.

"I didn't. I'm just heading to the toilet." Danny points towards the door that sits to my left.

"Oh, right. Still on for dinner tonight?"

"Hell yes I am. Look, I'm desperate for a pee. I'll be right back."

Danny rushes into the toilet, so I wait outside the studio to be invited in. A few minutes later, Danny returns and ushers me into the studio where I see everything setup just like it was before.

"Hey, Harry!" Kevin calls over to me.

"Hello," I reply.

I'm not quite sure what today's photoshoot entails, so as far as I'm aware, it's just a general shoot. There's no particular story I've been asked to share. I awkwardly wait by the door, anticipating someone to call me over to position myself in front of the camera. At that moment, when I'm lost in my thoughts, Kevin's gruff voice startles me and brings me back to life. I wheel myself over to the setup and position myself in front of the camera before being told what poses to do.

·•❤•❤•❤•❤•❤•

The nightlife in London is so pretty. Tall buildings glow like a row of Christmas trees, while the roads are buzzing with vehicles driving back and forth to their desired locations. Danny holds my hand as I wheel myself along the pavement using my other. We're headed towards a Mexican restaurant, which is brightly lit in the distance.

"You did well today," says Danny, "I really enjoyed doing your photoshoot."

"I bet you did," I say with a light chuckle and a wink. Once again, I was asked to take my shirt off for the photoshoot, so I guess they're trying to milk the 'you can do anything even if you are disabled' story. Which, although I know it's *true* - you really can do anything despite having a disability - I don't want them using my situation as some kind of money making scheme for the company.

Danny giggles. "Yes, you are very handsome underneath your shirt, but I do mean the photoshoot itself. It was fun."

"I know, I'm just messing with you."

As we make our way up the road towards the restaurant, Danny stops midway, causing me to make an abrupt stop too.

"Is everything okay?" I ask.

"Not really," says Danny.

I look up at him, confused. "What's wrong?"

For a few moments, he doesn't say anything. Instead, he crouches down and gently caresses my face before leaning in to give me a soft, meaningful kiss directly on the lips. I get lost in the moment and forget where I am as we both share this intimate moment. His lips are soft and gentle, and his thin layer of stubble above his top lip feels somewhat calming against my lips. He pulls away and stares at me, still holding my face.

"Sorry," he says, "I just couldn't resist. I've been wanting to kiss you from the moment we met, and what a better romantic setting than in a beautifully lit London city."

I smile, speechless. He's just the best, and I don't know what to say. I lean forward to kiss him again.

"I really like you," I confess.

"And I really like you too. Shall we go get food?"

I nod, a wide grin stretching across my face. "Yes, let's get food."

·♥·♥·♥·♥·♥·

The restaurant we go into is dimly lit, orange lamps hanging from the ceiling and LED lights screwed into the back border of the booths. A kind waitress shows us to our table and sets a menu down in front of each of us.

"I'll be back to take your order shortly," she says with a friendly smile.

Danny and I browse through the menu, eyes flicking back and forth between the many food choices presented to us on the large sheet of paper. My eyes keep darting between the spiced chicken burger, and the chicken fajita wraps. I'm always that difficult person in a restaurant who can't make his mind up what to get.

"Not sure what to get," says Danny, "what're you getting?"

I giggle. "I don't know either, I'm debating between a burger and the fajitas."

His face goes from a look of indecisiveness to a look of lust. "Ooh, fajitas. Love those. Maybe we could get two different types and share?"

"Yeah, that will be nice."

I look at the options on the menu. All the fajitas are chicken, except for the vegetarian option, and they all come with a variety of vegetables and sauces. In the end, we choose to get one lot of fajitas with a mild salsa sauce and barbecue flavouring, and another set of fajitas with sour cream sauce and roasted tomato flavouring. The waitress takes our order, as well as our choice of milkshakes as our drinks, and then heads off to the kitchen.

"So, when do you get your prosthetic?" Danny asks me.

"Next week," I reply. "A little nervous, but also very excited."

"Oh, amazing! I can imagine you're nervous, especially since you've been so reliant on your wheelchair for so long. Will probably be strange walking again."

"It definitely will. I've grown so used to the chair that I'm a little bit scared to say goodbye to it."

Danny nods sympathetically. "You don't have to say goodbye to it completely, though. You can still have it as a 'just in case' so if you ever do feel like you need it to help you around, then at least it's there. Better to have it and not need it, than to need it and not have it: that's what my mum always says."

"Yeah, I guess you're right." I look up and smile as our waitress returns to our table with our milkshakes.

"One strawberry milkshake," she says, placing it down in front of Danny, "and one banana milkshake." She places the glass in front of me, before rushing off through the bustling restaurant. People around us chatter loudly, making it difficult for Danny and I to hear each other a lot of the time. It takes around half an hour for our food to arrive, but when it does, it looks and smells *amazing*. The gentle sizzle of the chicken on the hot plate fuzzes in my ears, and the scent of it immediately makes my mouth water.

"Oh my god," I say, "this smells amazing!"

I let Danny take the first wrap and fill it with the chicken and vegetables, spreading the salsa dip across the fillings before wrapping it up like a burrito. I do the same thing and we both tuck in, appreciating the taste of Mexico.

By the time we've finished eating, my mouth feels like it's on fire. The salsa sauce was hotter than I expected, and mixed with the roasted tomato flavoured chicken, it made it even spicier. So, between each spicy fajita wrap, I had to have one with the sour cream sauce to eliminate the spices.

"I'm full now," I say, rubbing my belly. "Couldn't eat another thing."

"Not even dessert?" Danny quizzes, a teasing smirk on his face.

"Oh, go on then!" I let out a laugh, and the waitress comes over to clear our table.

"Can I get you anything else?" she asks.

"Could we have the dessert menu please? Oh, and a second round of milkshakes?"

"Of course. Same flavours as before?"

"Yes please."

She gives us both a friendly smile and a nod of her head before walking off towards the kitchen once again. This date night has been the most perfect experience, and I hope it will finish off nicely with cuddles and a movie on the sofa when we get back to Danny's flat. We agreed that I'd sleep in Danny's bed and he would sleep on the air bed. I wasn't keen on taking his bed for the night, but he insisted. So, I didn't argue against it. Instead, I took him up on his offer.

The waitress returns with the dessert menus and two milkshakes. "I'll be back in about five minutes."

·♥·♥·♥·♥·♥·

Back at Danny's flat, I get myself settled in the bed whilst Danny still tries to figure out the best position to sleep on the air bed.

"Are you sure you don't want to sleep in your own bed?" I ask.

"No, no," says Danny, "you are more than welcome to sleep in my bed. This air bed isn't the easiest thing to sleep on anyway, so I'd rather it be me than you sleeping on it."

Danny continues to toss and turn on the air bed, almost sliding off of it a few times. I've had enough of watching him struggle, so I come straight out and say it before I change my mind - "Do you want to share the bed? If you're adamant about me sleeping on the air bed, and you're *clearly* struggling with it yourself, then-"

"Okay, fine," replies Danny.

I can sense he's trying to act cool about my offer, but really, I can tell that he's actually pleased and rather excited by it. I shuffle over so he can slide in next to me. Before he can position himself properly, I lean into his chest and cuddle him tightly.

"Thank you for a great evening," I say.

Danny comfortably wraps his arms around me and kisses my forehead. "You're most welcome. I think you are absolutely amazing and you deserve a nice night out."

I look up at him and smile, before pushing myself up and leaning in to kiss his soft lips. This man is perfect.

Will

It's my first day back at the studio since my suspension, and I'm feeling somewhat nervous about seeing Danny again. I know we agreed to put things behind us, and I'm glad he's found a way to forgive my behaviour, but I can't help but feel anxious about seeing him again. I haven't seen him nor spoken to him since he showed up to my flat last week, so I'm just hoping he hasn't changed his mind since we spoke.

"Good morning," I say to the lady at reception. I don't recognise her: she must be new. She gives me a gentle smile and then gets back to tapping away on her keyboard. The phone rings in the distance as I walk through the double doors towards the staircase. Entering the staff room, everyone's attention turns to me. They don't say anything at first, instead giving me looks of disgust. Why did I have to behave like that?

"Hey," I say loudly, ensuring everyone can hear me. "How are you all?"

No one replies. Instead, they get back to their usual morning chitter-chatter without including me. I go through to the locker area where I bump into Danny closing his locker door and turning the key to secure it shut.

"Oh," he says, slightly surprised, "hey."

"Hey," I reply. "You okay?"

Danny nods, an uneasy and forced smile on his face. "Yeah. Just a little nervous about working with you again, not gonna lie."

"Honestly," I take a deep breath. "Me too. But, we're putting it all behind us, right?"

Danny pauses for a brief moment. "Right. But I *have* asked Stacey not to put us together on any shoots. We should just take this one step at a time."

He brushes past me and I take a moment to compose myself. Does everyone here really hate me now? Does Danny secretly still hate me? He's a difficult one to read sometimes. I put my things away in my locker and then head back into the staff room. I put the kettle on and offer everyone a round of tea, but they all decline - all except Danny.

"I guess we should at least make an effort to get along," says Danny. "And you can start making things up to me by making me a nice hot chocolate."

I smile. "Of course."

His smile seems kind of flirtatious. Am I reading it wrong? Or is he genuinely trying to flirt with me? I keep myself composed, so not to freak him out. If there is anything there between us, I'll let him make the first move. I pour hot water over the hot chocolate powder in Danny's mug, give it a stir and then hand it to him. He takes it from me and then sits down next to our colleagues on the sofa.

Stacey enters the room and takes me aside. "Keep away from Danny."

"He wants to make amends," I argue.

"I don't care. He doesn't deserve what you did, and now he's got himself a lovely boyfriend, I don't want you to mess things up."

Did I hear that right? *Boyfriend?* Since when did he have a boyfriend?

"Fine," I grunt.

Stacey walks away and my eyes follow her until they stop on Danny. Was he pretending to flirt with me earlier to get me on side? If this whole boyfriend thing is true, then I most certainly *will* mess it up. He's messed me around one too many times.

·♥·♥·♥·♥·♥·

"Hey, Danny!" I call when I walk through the canteen at lunchtime.

He turns around and smiles when he sees me approach him. "Hey."

"How's your boyfriend?" I ask, wrapping my arm around his shoulders.

He chuckles, shyly. "I don't have a boyfriend. Well, not quite."

"What do you mean?"

"We've not made it official yet."

"Well, maybe you should. Ask him to be your boyfriend."

Danny looks at me. "You think I should?"

I nod, and twist him to face me, holding onto his shoulders. "Absolutely! You like him? Go for it. So, who is he?"

When Danny goes quiet, I know who he's talking about. I had a feeling it was Harry, but I wanted Danny to confirm it.

"That freak of a model?" I hiss.

"Freak? What exactly is it about him that makes him a freak?" Danny snaps back.

I laugh. "Well, he's not exactly model material is he? He's in a wheelchair and will end up having a metal leg like he's some kind of bloody robot!"

"Don't you *dare* talk about him like that!"

"What you gonna do, Danny? Hit me?"

I look over my shoulder and see Stacey walking past in the distance. Annoyingly, she doesn't see Danny and

I arguing. All I need is for Danny to assault me, Stacey to witness it, and then he's out. And I'll be back in a job properly, with proper friends like I did before.

"You'd like that, wouldn't you?" Danny argues. "But I'm not going to give you the satisfaction."

Danny storms off, leaving me standing in the middle of the canteen with nothing but the muffled sound of the radio to keep me company. I've got to do something to get Danny out of here.

At the end of our lunch break, I head to my office and look at the bookings for the photoshoots. I see that Harry is booked in for tomorrow, just enough time for me to put my plan into place. If Danny and Harry have a huge bust-up, there is *no* chance Harry will accept Danny's proposal to be his boyfriend.

Danny

W<small>HEN</small> I <small>ARRIVE AT</small> the studio, I look around in disgust at what I see. My face burns up, eyes trying to push out angry tears, but I manage to hold them back. I rip one of the posters down and hold it in my clenched fists, watching the sides of the paper crease up. The words typed in bold typeface slap me in the face.

My boyfriend is a robot!

I read the words over and over again, and look at the photo of Harry taking pride of place in the centre of the poster. I grip harder onto the poster before screwing it up into a tight ball and launching it across the corridor.

The screwed up piece of paper lands at the feet of someone exiting the photography studio and I look up to see Will's smug face looking down at the now creased poster.

"This was you, wasn't it?" I hissed. "You're an absolute dickhead, you know that?"

Will chuckles. "What was me? Sorry, I have *no* idea what you're talking about." His sarcastic, jolly tone tells me all I need to know.

"If you don't take these posters down *now*, then I'm reporting you - again!"

Will pushes his bottom lip out, pretending to look sad. "Aww, are you worried your boyfriend is going to see what you *really* think about him?"

"I don't think anything of the *sort* about him! This is your handy work. Take them down, now!"

My raging tone attracts an audience, including Stacey. She hurries over and stands between Will and I.

"What's going on?" she asks, strictly.

I point at Will. "Have you seen the posters he's put up?"

Stacey shakes her head, confused. "No, I haven't. What posters?"

I pick up the screwed up poster from the floor, unfold it, and show it to her. "He's trying to make me look bad in front of Harry when he comes in for his photoshoot in..." I look at my watch... "five minutes."

Stacey looks up at Will, a horrified look on her face. "How could you do this, Will?"

Will holds his arms up, defensively. "I didn't do anything. Danny told me yesterday he thinks Harry's a freak and when he gets his metal leg, all he will be able to think of is the Terminator." Will chuckles at his own comment, not caring that nobody else finds him funny.

"Is that true?" a voice behind me says.

I turn around to find Harry sitting in his chair, glaring at me with puppy dog eyes, clearly hurt by what Will said. I really hope he believes me over Will.

"No," I say, "no, of course not. Will's being his usual self and trying to cause trouble. I think so highly of you, Harry."

Harry forces a gentle smile on his face. "So, what are these posters about?" He holds up three posters that he's ripped down from the walls on his way in.

"Again, that was Will's doing. I had nothing to do with that. He's jealous of us, jealous he can't have me because you're getting me."

Will laughs. "Oi, get a room lads."

"Shut up!" I scream. "I have had *enough* of your bullshit!"

Stacey holds me back to prevent me from slapping Will. "Calm down, Danny. You don't want to aggravate this. Maybe you should go home, and come back fresh faced tomorrow. Harry, you go too. I don't think it's a good idea for you to be here with Will." Stacey turns to look at Will. "And you...oh, just piss off."

Stacey walks away, leaving us all to it. I glare at Will for a few moments before turning on my heel and walking away before I get even more aggravated. Harry comes after me, but stops at the stairs.

"Danny, wait," he calls.

I turn around and look up at him from halfway down the stairs. "I'm sorry."

Harry heads over to the lift so I make my way over to a table and sit there whilst I wait for Harry to come back down in the lift. When he arrives, he joins me at the table.

"Why are you sorry?" he asks, taking hold of my hands. "You shouldn't be sorry."

I shake my head. "I'm sorry for what Will said. He's trying to get between us because he's jealous. You're getting the person that he can't have and he hates to see it happening in front of his very eyes."

"I get it. But, maybe we shouldn't see each other for a while."

A pit forms in my stomach. "What?"

"There's too much drama in your life for me to handle right now. I'm getting my prosthetic in a few days so I need to focus on that and my recovery. This business between you and Will is getting too much for me."

"Harry, please..."

"Don't beg," he interrupts. "I will call you when I'm ready. But right now, please just leave me alone."

Harry wheels himself out of the studio and around the corner in the car park. I sit at the table for a few minutes, shocked by what Harry has just done. Does he seriously want to call things off all because of a stupid thing Will said that only *he* thinks? I run out to the car park, catching up with Harry.

"Don't do this," I call. "Look, come back to mine and we can talk properly."

Harry huffs as he turns around in his chair. "Danny, please respect what I'm asking."

"I will, honestly. I just…I just want to understand. Let me grab my things and we can head back to mine?"

Reluctantly, Harry agrees. I head back indoors to get my belongings and then we meet back out in the car park. I take Harry to my car and we take the short drive back to my flat where we sit in silence for a few minutes while the kettle boils. Things have never been *this* awkward between us in the short time that we've known each other. I make us both a hot chocolate and then sit down on the sofa.

"I really like you," I say. "Whatever Will thinks isn't a reflection on what *I* think. He's a dick, and you shouldn't listen to him."

"It's just what he said about me being a freak and looking like the Terminator," Harry mumbles. "It really hurt my feelings."

I try to lighten the mood. "Hey, the Terminator is pretty cool, though."

Harry doesn't appreciate my attempt at a joke and shoots me a glare of distaste instead. "Not when it's being used as an insult to my disability. Danny, I know we haven't known each other long, but I do really like you too. But, something has to give. If we're going to give things a go, I don't want to be a model for this magazine anymore. Not while Will is working there, anyway. And I doubt he'll be fired...again."

"What are you trying to say?" I ask.

Harry pauses for a moment. "Come back down south with me. Move back in with your parents and we can do things properly. Otherwise, we won't see each other again as I'm not going to be coming to London."

It takes me a moment to understand what Harry is requesting me to do. He's asking me to give up my apprenticeship for him, a boy I've only known a couple of weeks.

"I-" I pause.

Harry stares at me. "I know it's a lot to ask, and I fully understand if you wish to stay. But, with or without you, I'm going back home and staying there. I'm quitting modelling for *Rainbow Gazette* with immediate effect."

I close my eyes, thinking extremely hard about the decision I need to make. On the one hand, this apprenticeship is my dream job and is something I've always worked hard towards. But on the other hand, Harry is right. Will is a toxic colleague and I can't work alongside him. When I open my eyes again, I look up at Harry and smile at him. I move in closer, gently cradle his face, and softly kiss him.

"I'll quit," I say.

· ♥ · ♥ · ♥ · ♥ · ♥ ·

"I'm quitting my apprenticeship," I say.

"What?" Mum sounds extremely disappointed on the other end of the phone. "But this is what you've always wanted."

"I know." I let out a sad sigh. "But there's this one guy who works there who is making it really intolerable to work there. I want to come home."

Mum stays silent for a few moments before speaking again. "I understand. I'm disappointed, and of course I'm gutted for you, but I understand. So, when are you coming home?"

"Hopefully at the weekend. I'll quit with immediate effect." In all honesty, I don't know if I will be able to quit with immediate effect, but at this point in time, I don't really care. They can't force me to stay.

"Okay, well I will let you have a long think about what you want to do and I'll speak to you soon, love," says Mum. "Goodnight, love you."

"Bye, love you too," I reply.

Mum ends the call and then it's just me in the flat again. Harry left a couple of hours ago to get his train home. We talked for hours about what we wanted, and we came to the conclusion that growing as people is a priority, and doing it *together* is what we want. We discussed what we could both do going forward, and he suggested that I sell my photos online on the website *Photos2U*, a stock image site that hundreds, if not *thousands*, of people use daily. It'd be great for exposure, and it will be exciting to see if any of my photography ends up on book covers, in magazines, or even on promotional material for businesses. I also did some research into how I could sell my photos physically, and I discovered a small cafe located on the outskirts of my town that often displays canvas prints on the wall and sells them to customers who express an interest. It could earn me a lot of money, so it is definitely something I could consider as a little pocket money earner while I look for a new job.

Harry and I also discussed what *he* would do going forward but he said that he's going to be focusing on his recovery before looking for a job. The modelling gig at *Rainbow Gazette* was, in his words, "a distraction" and something to keep him busy, but after the first session, he discovered it wasn't really his thing, and he only continued to do it so he could keep seeing me. He says modelling is still the route he wants to take, but maybe just in a different format - and maybe in a few years when he's become more confident with his body and the way his life has changed so quickly.

I pick up my phone and send a quick text to Harry, thanking him for helping me come to a decision about my current situation and being there for me. I never thought I'd quit a job for a guy, but if it means I can date someone in peace without someone constantly being there and pestering me, then I'll do it. And I *am* doing it.

Harry

THANK YOU FOR THIS afternoon. I'm going to email Stacey with my intention to leave with immediate effect in the morning, and ask to have a brief meeting with her. But I will not be working tomorrow and I'm going to make that very clear. Hope you're home safe xxx

I smile as I read the message that comes through on my phone from Danny. When we spoke about it earlier, I made it clear to him that I don't want to influence any decisions he makes and I want it to be his - and *only* his - decision. My guidance helped him make that decision, but overall, he made the final choice. I do think it is the *right* choice as the workplace isn't very positive at all. Will is a dick, Stacey's a bit overbearing - lovely, but overbearing. And the rest of the staff, while all lovely, seem to not want to be there. So, I'm glad that we've both made the decision to quit our roles there. Although mine is freelance so it doesn't make much difference to the company, Danny's is full-time, so it could potentially have an effect on the company.

Almost home, just waiting for the bus to arrive at the train station. I'm glad you managed to make the decision that's right for you. See you soon and hope you sleep well xx

I tuck my phone into my pocket as the bus arrives. The driver opens the door and lowers the ramp for me to get on, scan my pass, and then secure myself in the seating area specifically for wheelchair users.

The bus rumbles through the lit city, the moon shining from the pitch black sky through the front window of the bus. When my stop is announced over the speaker, I press the button to alert the driver I want to get off.

It's almost 9pm when I arrive home, the latest I've ever come home on my own in the wheelchair. Mum and Dad have already gone to bed, so I don't bother shouting up to them to let them know I'm home - they probably heard the door slam shut, anyway. I head to my bedroom and switch on my bedside lamp which dimly lights the room, creating a warm and intimate sensation that my big ceiling light just wouldn't do. It eases my tired eyes while I undress and roll under my duvet, the chilly autumnal breeze wafting through the tiniest gap between my window and its frame making me shiver.

I'm woken up by the crash of thunder and the rain hammering against my bedroom window. I roll onto my side and check my phone - 6:30.a.m.

I grunt and close my eyes again, trying my best to force myself back to sleep. But the weather outside is keeping me awake. A flash of lightning glows through my eyelids, lighting up the darkness for a few seconds. I pull the duvet over my head to block out the flashing sky and the claps of thunder.

I must have dozed off because the next thing I know, it's 8:15.a.m. Mum crashes into my room, hurrying me to get out of bed. When I realise what day it is, I throw myself into my wheelchair and head to the kitchen. Today, I get my prosthetic leg.

"Your appointment is in one hour, you should have been up ages ago!" Mum shouts. "Why didn't you set an alarm?"

"I did, but I must have slept through it," I say. "The thunder woke me up stupidly early."

Mum rolls her eyes. "Next time, stay awake." She lets out a light chuckle.

I quickly scoff my breakfast and then brush my teeth in the downstairs bathroom. Looking in the wall length mirror, I look down at my stump. Although I've learned to live with it, it's still a struggle to come to terms with the fact I'll never have my leg back. I just hope that Danny still likes me for who I am in years to come.

Mum and I arrive at the hospital just in time for my appointment. Dad was meant to come with us but he got called into an emergency meeting at work. The consultant invites us into his office and introduces himself - I've never seen him before.

"I'm Doctor Chapman," he says. "Your usual consultant is off sick with a virus, so I'm taking over her appointments for the week. I hope that's okay?"

I nod. "Fine with me."

"Excellent. So, Harry, your prosthetic is ready and I'm referring you to a physiotherapist to start sessions as soon as possible to help you progress quickly with your new leg."

I look over at Mum nervously and she smiles at me, gripping my hand. This is a brand new start for me, and I can't wait to tell Danny all about it.

·˙♥˙·♥˙·♥˙·♥˙·♥˙·

I arrive home with Mum and I head to my room to charge my phone for a little bit before I text Danny. Mum and I sit down at the kitchen table and tuck into the KFC that she bought on the way home for us to have for lunch. We talk about the appointment and what my feelings are about the next few weeks, and what Mum's feelings are too. I tell her that I'm looking forward to it all - my life will finally be getting back on track.

It's late afternoon when Danny finally responds to my text.

I told Stacey I'm quitting. I'll be coming back home this weekend, so we can go on another date night. Xx

A smile gently stretches across my face. As much as I don't want Danny to quit his apprenticeship for me, it's clear that it is what's best for him. He clearly hates it there. Will's attitude was horrible, and Danny is better off out of there. I sent him a list of local cafes that take in local photographers' images and sell them on behalf of the photographer. Each cafe takes a royalty from the sale, but the photographer gets the majority of the sale cost, and I hope that Danny takes that on as a pocket-money earner until he finds himself a job that he can do full time.

That's great! I hope you aren't just doing it for me though. Xx

My biggest regret if things ever went tits up between Danny and I would be that I dragged him away from London just because *I* didn't like Will. I know Danny doesn't like him either, but our blossoming relationship is definitely playing a huge part in him leaving London and coming back home.

No, it is definitely what's best for me. I want us to grow a relationship together. And the only way we can really do that is if we're close-by. Xx

Danny

I can't believe I finally did it. Stacey was shocked to hear that I'm leaving my apprenticeship and want to return home, but she also understands *why*. I can't work alongside Will, no matter how hard I try. He makes me too uncomfortable and I want to make things work between Harry and I. In order to do that, I need Will out of my life for good.

"Sorry to hear that you want to leave," Stacey says, "but I do wish you all the best for whatever is next to come for you. I hope no one has made you feel pushed out, other than Will of course?"

"No, not at all. But, to be honest, working here isn't really for me. I'm not doing much, I feel like a spare part, and I'm not being treated like one of the team. Just because I'm an apprentice, it doesn't mean everyone can treat me like an outsider. I'm no different to the rest of them."

Stacey nods. "I understand. Of course, you will be paid for the time you have worked here, and I gather you understand that you need to vacate your flat within the next five days?"

"Yes, I'll be going home this weekend."

"Well, Danny, it has been a pleasure." Stacey holds her hand out and I take her up on her offer of a handshake.

I smile and leave the room, gathering my things and then departing the building one last time. I look back and see Will lingering by a window. Out of pure pettiness, I stick my middle finger up at him, and then head over to my car, chuckling on my way.

When I arrive back at the flat, I throw myself on the sofa. Despite it being a nice, sunny day, I don't want to spend the day outside. I only have a few days until the weekend, so I should probably spend them packing my stuff, ready to return home. I'm glad I kept the boxes from when I moved up here because I can just put everything back in and not worry about finding new boxes.

For ten minutes, I lounge on the sofa, staring at the wall in front of me in silence, except for the busy flow of traffic in the distance. I stand up, and grab the boxes from my storage cupboard. I have no idea where to begin - what should I pack, what do I need for the next few days?

My phone pings and I pick it up, looking at who has sent me a message. It's Harry. I open the message and smile as I read it. He's so excited for me to return home so we can properly build a relationship. I've never met anyone like him before, and he makes me genuinely so happy. I just can't believe that Will tried to get between us, especially with that *stupid* poster about Harry being a robot.

Shit. I've only just remembered that today was Harry's appointment to get his prosthetic leg. I don't even acknowledge the message he sent me, as I'm desperate to know how his appointment went. I put my phone back down on my bed and I head over to the living area and start packing away the things I don't need such as the framed photos and my ornamental pieces. Already, the flat starts to feel empty of all my belongings. I'll be sad to leave London behind, but it is what's best for me. Harry sent me a list of cafes in my area that sell photos on behalf of photographers and take a small royalty. I've also been researching online photo selling platforms, and I've written a list of potential good ones, so I should be okay for money, providing that people buy my photos until I find a new job.

·♥·♥·♥·♥·♥·

I finished most of my packing a couple of hours ago, and I've just been laying on my bed, messaging Harry back and forth all afternoon. I told him that once I'm home, I'll sort out my bedroom, spend Saturday evening with my parents, and then I'll see him on Sunday evening. As much as I'd love to see him earlier, I need to make time to see Ellie. I haven't had much chance to speak to her since I left for London, and all my online time has been spent messaging Harry. So, I want to spend the day with her on Sunday.

We've made plans to go to the cinema and then Wetherspoons for lunch. It'll be the first time we've seen each other in a few months, so we don't want to do anything too extravagant. Plus, Christmas is just five weeks away and we will most likely have a big party like we do every year. So, we're going to be saving money for that.

I can't wait to see you again. It's been so long! Plus, I want all the juicy gossip about you and your new fella x

I smile at Ellie's message and I type out my reply. Although I haven't spoken to Ellie much, the one thing I've spoken about the *most* with her is Harry. But, I haven't told her all about him - just the simple things. She doesn't know the details of our dinner date, the night we spent together, or any of the lovey-dovey stuff. All she knows is that I met him at work and we bonded almost straight away. I didn't tell her about Will - that story can wait until I see her.

After I've finished my dinner, I settle down for the evening to watch television on my own. Just as I turn on my favourite comedy series, my phone rings. Harry's name pops up on the screen and I swipe the green phone icon to answer the call.

"Hey," I say.

"Hey," says Harry, "you alright?"

"Yeah, I'm good, thanks. You okay?"

Harry clears his throat. "I'm all good. Just felt like calling you, wanted to hear your voice."

"That's cute. I'm sorry I didn't reply to your text, I've been so busy this afternoon packing all my bits that it didn't occur to me to reply."

"It's okay. I'd rather talk to you about the appointment than text, anyway. How did it go with Stacey today?"

I'd rather not talk about it to be honest, but it is clear that Harry wants to deter the conversation away from his appointment. Did it really go that bad? I tell Harry all about the chat I had with Stacey, my reasoning for leaving and why I don't feel appreciated enough. Harry listens to every word I speak with content and offers me verbal comfort when I get a bit upset about it all. After all, it's a huge decision I've made and I'm basically throwing my dream away because it is unlikely something like this could come up again any time soon.

We chat for hours and before I know it, it's ten to midnight. I tell Harry goodnight and then I settle down to sleep. After having such a long chat with him - probably the longest we've ever spoken for in a single sitting - I realised that I *have* made the right decision about the apprenticeship, and moving back home is the best thing that I can do. This might sound crazy, especially as Harry and I have only known each other for a few weeks, but I think I'm falling for him. He's the best guy I've met in a long, long time and he treats me well. He gets me - we get *each other* - and that's why we get on so well.

I decide I'm going to ask him to be my boyfriend officially when I move back home. Things need to progress further, and that is definitely the next step.

Part 3

Danny

I ARRIVED HOME ABOUT an hour ago, after a pretty clear journey on the roads. My bedroom is a tip at the moment as I haven't had much of a chance to sort out my things, but it feels good to be back where I belong. Mum and I sit at the kitchen table, talking things through and helping her understand why I left my apprenticeship. She's horrified to learn about Will and all the horrid things he put me through, a little hurt by me not telling her sooner.

"I'm sorry," I say. "I didn't want to worry you, that's all. I thought he'd get over it, but clearly not."

Mum rubs my hand. "At least you're home and safe now."

I nod, and Dad walks into the room. "Safe? What are you safe from?"

I look up at Mum, my eyes pleading with her not to say anything to him. Although Dad kind of came to terms with me being gay just before I left for London, I have a feeling that he may not still be one hundred percent with it, and will probably laugh off my situation. Either that, *or* he would travel to London himself, find Will and threaten to kill him. Either way, I don't want Dad knowing.

"Nothing," says Mum, honouring my plea, "it's just one of those sayings. Doesn't necessarily mean anything."

Dad shrugs and walks over to the kettle to make himself a cup of coffee. Before Mum and I can say anything else that lets my dad overhear our conversation, I head up to my room and start sorting out my things. I look around my room, not knowing where to start nor remembering where anything went before.

Just as I open my suitcase to begin unloading, my phone rings. It's Ellie.

"Hey," I say, holding the phone up to my ear.

Ellie and I chat for a good half hour, making sure we're still on for our day out tomorrow. We decide to just go to McDonalds for lunch instead of Wetherspoons, and we're going to watch a new *Disney* film that's just been released in the cinema. Once I end the phone call, I start unpacking my bags, ignoring my phone every time it pings. I worry that some of the messages could be from Harry, thinking I'm ignoring him. It's tempting to reply to him just so he knows I'm okay, but I decide that getting my stuff sorted is my priority and I can't get distracted by anything else.

·♥·♥·♥·♥·♥·

The autumnal rain hammers against my bedroom window, waking me before my alarm goes off. A distant rumble of thunder, a vicious flash of lightning. I turn over and look at the time displaying on my phone screen.

5:30.a.m.

I roll over with a grunt and try to go back to sleep. But no matter what I try, the weather is keeping me awake. I don't need to be up for another three hours at least, so this is really taking the piss right now. Admitting defeat, I roll out of bed and head to the bathroom. I don't flush the toilet as it is still early, and then I head back to bed. I lay as still as I can, keeping my eyes shut tight. I block out the noise coming from outside, drifting into deep thoughts and soon into a deep sleep again.

When I wake up again, my alarm is screaming in my ear. I switch it off and lay still in my bed for a few minutes, staring at the ceiling whilst letting out the occasional yawn. My first night back in my own bed was amazing, and I'm glad I made the right decision coming home. There's just something about home comforts.

I check through my social media, checking for any messages and notifications. I don't have anything yet. Harry must still be asleep, and Ellie is probably only just waking up now. We agreed to get up at around the same time so we can spend the morning planning our afternoon properly before I pick her up and head into town. Just then, a message pops up at the top of my screen.

Good morning, sleeping beauty. Hope your first night back at home was bliss! Xxx

A smile stretches across my face without any encouragement. Harry never fails to make me smile and that's why I like him so much. Maybe I'm falling for him. I feel like it's too soon to have those feelings, but he is just so perfect in every way.

Hey, yes I had a great night's sleep, except for the thunder waking me up at 5.a.m. How are you getting on with your prosthetic?

Harry responds pretty quickly, telling me how his physio appointments are going and the progress he's making. I'm so pleased that he is recovering fairly quickly considering he was always sure he was going to struggle getting to grips with his new way of living. We chat on and off for a good half hour before Ellie finally messages me, confirming our plans are still on for today.

Tiredly, I roll out of bed, pull my oversized jumper over my head, and head downstairs. I open the living room curtains and see that it is still miserable outside, the road as black as the night sky from all the wetness, and the rain still hammering down, causing ripples in puddles and drops trickling down the window as if it is crying. I watch the elderly lady from up the road walking her toy poodle, both wearing bright yellow raincoats to bring some sunshine to this rainy day. After a few minutes of silently observing the weather, I head into the kitchen and make myself some breakfast, determined not to have a big one so that I can have my McDonald's *and* snacks in the cinema later.

Eleven o'clock rolls around quickly, and I head out to my car, holding my umbrella over my head to protect myself from the gloomy weather. I get in the car, send Ellie a quick message letting her know I'm on my way, and then I set off.

I arrive at Ellie's house fifteen minutes later, parking up in front of her driveway and waiting for her to come out to the car. As soon as I spot her front door opening out of the corner of my eye, I can't help but feel a bit of excitement. It's been months since I saw my best friend, and I'm really looking forward to spending the afternoon with her - and tell her all about Harry.

·♥·♥·♥·♥·♥·

I arrive home after spending all afternoon with Ellie, and tell Mum and Dad that I won't be staying for long as I'm meeting up with Harry for dinner. I hadn't intended to tell them much about him, but I figured that now that I'm back home and will be spending more time with him, I should probably tell my parents all about him.

"I'm happy you're happy," Dad says.

"I'm pleased for you, love," says Mum, a smile on her face.

Dad's acknowledgement, whilst accepting, didn't sound as convincing as Mum's. I know he's still not keen on the idea of me being gay and having a boyfriend, but at least he's trying. By the time I've finished having the conversation with Mum and Dad about Harry, I realise I'm going to be late meeting him. I send him a quick text, letting him know I'm on my way, and then hurry out of the house.

I pull up outside Harry's house. While I wait for him to come outside, I look at his front garden. It's beautiful. A gravel path leads up to the front door, with grass either side of it. Flowers decorate the border, with the occasional solar light in between. A bird table stands in the centre, a small robin perching on the edge and pecking away at the food that has been left in there.

A few moments later, Harry approaches my car. I hop out to help him into the car before folding his wheelchair down and putting it across the backseats.

"Hey," I reply.

He leans over and kisses me. I'm taken aback, not expecting him to greet me in such a way outside his home where his parents could be watching out the front window. But, I smile at him and kiss him back before shifting into gear and driving up the road.

"How was it with your friend today?" he asks.

"It was really nice," I say. "It's been months since I last saw Ellie so it was lovely seeing her again. Went to see that new *Disney* movie in the cinema."

"Oh, amazing! And how was your journey home yesterday?"

"It was great. Traffic was fairly good, made it back in one piece." I chuckle.

Harry falls silent and I realise what I just said. I briefly look over at him whilst my main focus is the road. "Shit, I'm so sorry. I didn't mean to say that, or mean for it to sound like I was making fun of your situation."

"No, no," says Harry, "it's fine. I know you didn't mean it in a nasty way. Just still a sensitive subject, that's all."

I pull up into the main car park for the precinct and park my car as close to the entrance as possible. Harry and I get out of the car and head towards the Nando's that is situated to the left of the cinema that's ahead of us.

"So, are you a mild spice gay, or a hot spice gay?" I joke.

"Mild, all the way," Harry says with a chuckle, "I'm a wimp when it comes to spices."

I laugh as we enter the restaurant and a waiter takes us to a table. We sit down and browse the menu, although I already know what I'm getting as I get the same thing every time I come here.

When I return from the payment counter, Harry and I sit in silence for a few moments, both unsure what to say to each other. I want to break the silence but I just can't think of anything to say other than "the weather out there is *awful*."

Number one rule of dating is to never talk about the weather, and I've already broken that rule. Harry brings up my apprenticeship again, and I assure him that I'm glad I've left and it was the right decision.

"Have you had anymore thought about the cafe that sells photos?" he asks.

"Yeah, I've thought about it a lot, actually," I say. "It's a great idea but it's not what I want to do at the moment. I feel like my photography needs to be on another level before I start trying to sell it to people to display in their home. I'm thinking about going travelling next year."

"Really? That's amazing!"

I nod. "Yeah, it's something I've always wanted to do. Italy, France, and America are the main countries I want to visit, but I wouldn't mind visiting Australia, Spain, and Iceland."

"You think it could help develop your career as a photographer too?"

"Most definitely." I sparkle slightly with joy. "There are so many opportunities for photography around the world, much better views and locations than here in the UK. I hope that maybe then, I'll have some photos actually worth selling."

Harry nods. "That makes sense. I guess a lot of your stuff is portraits anyway. No one wants a photo of a random person on their wall unless it's a celebrity."

Our food arrives and we chat in between bites. After telling Harry about my plans to travel, it's made me more excited about actually doing it. I had planned to do it on my own, but now I want Harry to come with me. We can make it a holiday, just the two of us. It will take us at least three months to do a tour of all the countries I intend to visit, but we can always extend that if we want to visit *more* countries.

"Come with me," I say.

"Come with you, where?" Harry asks.

"Travelling. When I go travelling next year, come with me."

Harry looks astounded, speechless. He doesn't say anything for a few moments as he gets his head around what I've just said.

"Did you really just ask me that?"

I nod. "It's not that big of a deal, calm down. I've not asked you to marry me!"

Harry chuckles. "I know, but next year isn't that far away, and we're not even officially boyfriends yet."

"Yet?"

Harry nods. "Yes, yet. We will be, but we aren't."

"I'm not intending to go until late spring, anyway, so there is plenty of time to get things in place."

I can see the cogs whirring in Harry's mind. He's giving me the impression that he does *want* to come with me. But something is holding him back.

Harry

Danny and I sit across from each other, discussing the fact he's just asked me to go travelling with him next year. We're not even at the holidaying together stage yet. I know he intends to go in the spring and summer, but thinking about it, that's not that far away.

My leg situation is holding me back from going. What if something goes wrong while we're in a completely different country? What if I'm not completely recovered? So many things can go wrong, and I'm petrified of it happening when my family aren't around to help me. But, I *really* want to go with Danny. How can I make a decision when there are so many reasons for going, yet so many more for *not* going?

"I think we should talk about it another time," I finally say. "It's a very big decision to make."

"Of course, yeah," says Danny. "I understand."

I fall silent, finishing off my food and waiting for our table to be cleared before we order dessert. That was the end of our conversation about going travelling together - I made it clear to Danny that I didn't want to talk about it anymore tonight.

"So, what do you fancy doing afterwards?" I ask, breaking the awkward silence.

Danny shrugs. "Not sure, that new bowling alley has opened up just round the corner. We could go there."

Bowling? I'm pretty crap at bowling, but it would be a fun date night if we play it.

"Sure," I say, "that sounds fun."

·♥·♥·♥·♥·♥·

The rest of the evening is pretty awkward. Danny and I barely speak after we leave Nando's, bowling is a quick twenty minute game, and then we agree to call it a night. This whole travelling malarkey has frazzled my brain. It would be great fun to go, but it will be a bad decision if things go tits up between us when we're halfway across the world.

I arrive home at 9:30pm. and Mum is waiting for me. She sees the look of distress on my face, and rubs my shoulder, offering me comfort. I take a deep breath and tell her all about the conversation Danny and I had.

"How do you feel about going?" she asks.

"I don't know," I reply. "On the one hand, it will be a great opportunity for us both, and also allows us to grow our relationship even more. But, on the other hand, if things go wrong, we're stuck together."

Mum nods, knowing exactly how I feel. "I remember when I was your age, maybe a bit younger. Before I met your dad, I was dating a guy called Tony. All the girls wanted him - he was tall, dark, and handsome."

"Cliche," I mutter.

"He asked me to go travelling around Europe with him. It was his dream to follow in his grandfather's footsteps, finish the grand tour of Europe that his grandfather had started but never got the chance to finish. I went with him, and we toured the whole of Europe in twelve months, doing all the mountain hikes, sightseeing... You name it, we did it."

I look at Mum, confused. "Where is this story going?"

"We got through it all, and our relationship survived. Granted, three months after we returned home, I broke up with with him because I found out he slept with one of the French girls we met on our tour around Paris, but that isn't the point."

"So what is the point?"

Mum sighs. "What I'm trying to say is that all relationships will have their ups and downs, whether you've been together for one week, one month, one year... You need to take these opportunities while you can. So what if you and Danny don't last throughout, or even some time afterwards. At least you can say that you *did* it. You *went* travelling, did something completely out of your comfort zone."

I give Mum a hug, telling her "Thank you," and then heading to bed. It's going to be a massive decision to make, one that I'm not going to make lightly. But Mum's pep-talk has given me food for thought, and is going to hopefully make my decision an easier one to make.

·♥·♥·♥·♥·♥·

I wake up to a text from Danny, apologising for freaking me out last night. My reply is pretty vague, but I tell him I'm okay and just need time to think. We don't talk for much of the morning, and the vast majority of my time is spent moping around at home, feeling sorry for myself, itching to tell Danny that I want to go travelling with him.

I made the decision last night as I was falling asleep that I do want to go. But I don't want to be too hasty in telling him, in case I change my mind. I need to be sure of my decision first before I tell him. I can't get his hopes up and then let him down.

The day passes by very slowly for me - I didn't have a lot to do. I found myself in a depressive slump, trying to get my head around such a huge decision that I'm being forced to make. But as the sun begins to set and the sky grows darker, I send Danny a risky text.

I'm going to come travelling with you next year.

Danny

IT TAKES ME SEVERAL times to read the text Harry has just sent me before I'm able to fully comprehend what he's told me. He *wants* to come travelling with me. Now that he's said for sure that he wants to, it has made me even more excited to go. It's not for a few months yet though, so I can't get my hopes up too much. He could change his mind at any moment.

OMG I'm so excited that you've said yes! Are you 100% sure you want to come? I don't want you to feel pressured.

I'm probably overthinking it, but I need to cover all bases. If he *is* feeling pressured, then I'd rather he be honest. However, if he does genuinely want to come, then I am thrilled.

Yes, I would love to come. I'll need to get a few things in place financially, but I defo want to come with you xx

A wave of excitement washes over me, and I do a little happy dance in my bedroom. Travelling next year is going to be *amazing*. Just me, my boy, and the world.

·♥·♥·♥·♥·♥·

As the sun rises over the south coast, I'm already awake. Once again, we had a night of storms, and now the weather is acting like it didn't have multiple moments of rage during the night. My curtains don't block out the light very well and I have to pull my duvet over my head to shield myself.

The frosty, winter sun floods my bedroom with light, casting shadows across every wall and surface. For a brief moment, it feels like it's providing my room with some heat. But then, as the sky becomes slightly overcast, the feeling of heat disappears and I'm shivering again.

I send Harry a good morning text, and ask if he wants to meet up again today. Now that he has agreed to come travelling with me, I feel like we should get the ball rolling and start making some basic plans, such as ideas of where we would like to visit. Obviously, they will just be ideas and nothing set in stone, especially as money - limited money - will be involved.

Harry and I meet up at lunch time. I ask if he wants to come back to mine so we don't spend money on food out again, but he insisted that he isn't ready to come to my house yet, especially as my parents will be there and he's not ready to meet them yet either. I completely respect that, so we go into the library where we can look at books about Europe, up-to-date maps, and get a drink and a bite to eat in the cafe.

Looking around the cafe, I notice the wall is plastered in photographs taken of local landmarks, historical buildings, and beautiful landscapes. Each one has a small price label underneath it with the name of the photographer and their signature. It gives me an idea, and I decide to browse the array of imagery while Harry finds us a table to sit at. By the window is a stand with a handful of leaflets secured inside. I take one, and read what it says.

Are you a local photographer? We're always looking out for new and current talent to display in our library cafe. Find our contact details below and get in touch!

I smile, and look behind me to find where Harry is sitting. I wander over to the table with the leaflet and place it down in front of him. Without saying a word, Harry nods his head and looks at me.

"You think I should do it?" I ask.

"One hundred percent. You've got the talent, you just need to build your portfolio of photos people will buy," says Harry.

"Travelling will give me that opportunity."

"No time like the present. This time next year, this cafe may not sell photos anymore. Or, they may not even be open. Take the opportunity now whilst you can. Tomorrow, you're going to start building your portfolio."

I don't argue. Harry's right - there is *no* time like the present and I should grab every opportunity that comes my way with open arms. So, I promise myself that tomorrow, I will start taking those photos and submitting them to the library cafe.

·♥·♥·♥·♥·♥·

It takes me a while to adjust my camera to the right settings for this new style of photography that I'm taking on. The lighting is so different to what I'm used to because natural lighting moves around constantly, whereas studio lighting is static. Harry sits on a bench, watching me work my magic and produce some (hopefully) beautiful shots of the landscapes that lay before us.

"How's it coming along?" Harry asks.

"So far," I say, "pretty good. Taking me a while to get used to completely new camera settings but I'm getting it."

"Perfect. There's so much here that will provide you with some great photo opportunities as well."

We're at a nature reserve in East Hampshire, the lake spreading for miles. The nature reserve is fairly quiet today with the exception of the odd dog walker and jogger who gives Harry and I a brief, friendly smile before continuing with their exercise routine.

A robin swoops down and lands on a branch in a perfect photo position. I position my camera, focus it and snap ten or so continuous shots before the robin eventually flies away, startled by the sound of my camera shutter. I quickly flick through the shots I took, impressed by their quality and the movements I managed to capture.

Harry and I continue our walk through the reserve, him limping next to me whilst intertwining his arm with mine. He's said his physio is going *really* well and he's making further progress than anyone expected. That's something I'm really pleased with because it means we can go on nice walks like this. We stop where the lake merges into the river that flows gently in the winter breeze. The water looks cold as it rushes over the few mounds of rocks that lay still underneath the water. I set my camera on the tripod, set a long shutter speed for approximately six seconds and let the camera do the rest of the work. I press my shutter, take a step back, and wait for the click to indicate that the photo has been taken. A quick look at the photo on my preview screen suggests to me that I need to have another go at the photo, decreasing the exposure and increasing the shutter speed. I play around with the settings until it is just right, and before I know it, I've produced a *stunning* shot.

"That looks incredible," beams Harry.

"Thank you," I say, a proud smile stretching across my face.

We continue our trek through the reserve, stopping to allow me to take more photos and just to admire the beauty of the nature that surrounds us. At this time of year, there isn't a huge amount of things to take the most stunning photo of because the trees are bare, animals are hibernating for the winter, and birds aren't laying eggs. I've been making do with what I've got, but I certainly hold no hopes over having any of the photos from *today* being featured in the library cafe.

At around half past twelve, Harry and I head back to the car and grab our picnic box and sit down at one of the benches that the birds have kindly decorated for us. I spread a blanket across the table so we've got a relatively hygienic surface to lay our food on, and then Harry begins unloading the box. Despite it being three degrees outside, Harry is warming my heart with his adorable smiles, and the way he digs around in the box to find the best snacks that we brought with us.

He truly is one in a million.

· ♥ · ♥ · ♥ · ♥ · ♥ ·

Our walk through the nature reserve lasted us all day because by the time we leave, everyone is starting to head home from work and the roads are as busy as the Saturday morning market downtown.

"Thanks for coming with me today," I say to Harry, rubbing his knee as we come to a standstill in the traffic.

"No, thank *you* for inviting me," Harry replies. "I really enjoyed today."

I kiss his cheek just as the traffic starts moving again, and the car behind gives me a brief honk of the horn before I move off in the flow of traffic. We'd spent all day talking to each other so our journey home is a quiet one, with very little to talk about. Mostly, we just reminisce on our day out, but other than that, we don't talk a lot on our way home.

Harry climbs out of my car and hobbles up his garden path that leads to his front door. He waves me off before his mum or dad can open the door and then I drive away, making my way home.

When I arrive home, I jump straight onto my computer and upload the photos I took today onto my USB stick. Then, I sift through them all, taking note of the image file names that I love the most that I want to edit and post on my social media.

I come across one photo - it's of a deer lounging in the sun next to the lake. Never did I ever think I would capture such a gorgeous photograph until now. I stare at it, noting down its file name, and then stare at it some more. The deer lays in the sun, staring directly at the camera, the bright light in the sky making its eyes squint.

What a shot!

Before I get too invested in this one photograph, I move onto the next, and then the next, and the next. Approximately ten minutes later, I've written a list of about fourteen photos I want to edit, and the rest will just stay as they are. I don't dare delete them, in case I want to come back to them one day and either just remember one of the best days ever, or if I need more photos to edit and post online.

As I open my editing software, my phone buzzes next to me on the table. It's a text from Harry.

Had a great day today, will be amazing to do it again soon. Can we meet for lunch tomorrow? There's something we need to talk about. Xx

Well, whatever it is that he wants to talk to me about, it can't be *that* bad if he wants to go for another day out again soon. But I can't help but worry about what it might be. So, I text him back asking for a clue.

You will have to wait and see! Xx

I roll my eyes - he's so secretive! I just hope that whatever it is, he isn't backing out of travelling with me next year.

·♥·♥·♥·♥·♥·

Harry and I meet up for lunch at *Wetherspoons* - typical, I know. We sit down, order our food and then we sit and chat for a while.

"So, what did you want to talk to me about?" I ask, before biting into my burger.

"Not here," says Harry. "We'll talk afterwards."

"You're not breaking the news to me that you're about to move to planet Mars are you?"

Harry chuckles. "No, no. I'm moving to the Moon." He winks at me.

I let out a gentle laugh. "Seriously, is it something bad?"

"Not at all. Well, for me, I don't think it's bad."

I honestly cannot help but wonder what it is he needs to talk to me about. Meeting up for lunch, and then can't tell me what it is? Is this...*the* moment?

We left *Wetherspoons* about ten minutes ago and now we're sat in the park across the road, shivering in the winter breeze. Harry cuddles into me and I wrap my arms around him to warm him up.

"So, this...thing," I say.

Harry looks up at me. "It's awkward. Well, not awkward. Just...scary."

"What is it?"

Harry pulls himself away from me and takes hold of my hands, looking at me dead in the eyes. An affectionate smile appears on his face before he leans in to kiss me.

"I've been wracking my brains for ages trying to figure out how to approach this," says Harry.

My heart begins to beat faster, hammering against my chest like it is trying to escape and intertwine itself with Harry's.

"But I need to just say it." Harry takes a deep breath. "I, err...I love you, Danny."

I tear up a little, glad that Harry was the first one to say it because I've been so scared to say it to him. But hearing him say it has made it a whole lot easier for me.

"I love you too," I say.

We embrace each other in a long kiss before landing into a cuddle again. I feel like I should ask him the next question.

"So..." I say. "Does that mean you want to be my boyfriend officially?"

Harry nods. "Yes. I would *love* to be your boyfriend."

Again, we kiss before heading back to my car to sit in the warm. We head to the beach and watch the waves crash against the rocks and slither up onto the sand. No words are said, we just sit next to each other in my car, holding hands in a romantic embrace.

I turn to him and look at his eyes, adoringly.

"I've never met anyone like you before," I say. "I'm so glad we met, I really do love you."

Harry doesn't say anything. Instead, he just smiles and squeezes my hand tighter. A true love story where boy meets boy isn't something that is often heard of in this world. During my time of online dating, nobody wants anything serious. It's just hookups, one night stands, endless numbers of guys saying "Yeah, let's go on a date," and then ghosting me or blocking me. Harry is the first guy I've met who actually wants something serious and I'll be forever grateful for that.

In a world where homophobia is still rife, mine and Harry's story will be stronger and hold more power than a homophobe ever will. Love is love, whether it's boy meets girl, girl meets girl, or boy meets boy. Love stories are all over, and the more we fight for justice, the better our chances.

"You're amazing," says Harry, finally. "I *really* love you."

About the Author

Jake Uniacke is an indie author from Hampshire, United Kingdom. He discovered his love and talent for writing at a very young age, and published his first short story in 2015 at the age of 14. As well as writing, Jake is also a photographer and specialises in nature, wildlife and landscape photography. His creative side has flourished over the years, which has helped him build a career using all the things he knows and loves.

Printed in Great Britain
by Amazon